"Sheldon Lee Compton's *Brown Bottle* is a sharply written story of a man scorched by circumstances but who embodies Harry Crews' dictum that survival is triumph enough. Compton articulates the real hardscrabble world of contemporary Kentucky Appalachia he so intimately understands, writing with a stark and powerful but emotionally subtle voice. Readers of Chris Offutt and Breece Pancake will have an accomplished new author to add to their shelves."

—Charles Dodd White, author of *A Shelter of Others* and *Sinners of Sanction County*

OTHER BOOKS BY SHELDON LEE COMPTON

The Same Terrible Storm: Stories, Foxhead Books 2012

Where Alligators Sleep: Stories, Foxhead Books 2014

BOTTOM DOG PRESS

BROWN BOTTLE

A NOVEL

SHELDON LEE COMPTON

APPALACHIAN WRITING SERIES
BOTTOM DOG PRESS
HURON, OHIO

© 2016 Bottom Dog Press, Inc.
ISBN: 978-1-933964-89-8
Bottom Dog Publishing
PO Box 425, Huron, Ohio 44839
http://smithdocs.net

First Edition

General Editor: Larry Smith
Layout: Susanna Sharp-Schwacke
Cover Design: Ryan W. Bradley

DEDICATION

For Heather, who gave me time, again and again.

"Fall seven times, stand up eight."
—Japanese Proverb

PROLOGUE

Brown learned to walk easy in his boots. Heel to toe, especially in the winter when he couldn't slip them off on the front porch.

He did this, heel to toe, because he lived with his sister, Mary, and she slept light. Brown had moved in four years ago when their mother died of natural causes before she turned sixty.

Died of natural causes.

Natural causes being a hard life that included lots of alcohol and lots of smoking. Natural causes being their daddy busted her up about twice a week.

Still, natural causes, the doctors said. And they believed them. Mostly the two of them wanted to believe because of sadness, and because Brown drank from one side of the clock to the other, and Mary didn't want to think about what killed their mother. She didn't really want to think about her dead. It wasn't entirely clear whether Mary cared if a hard life killed Brown or not. Brown was sure she looked at him and thought about death or about all the men who'd done nothing but wrong her.

Still, Brown tried to walk quiet late at nights while Mary slept. He thought the world of Mary. *Enough men in her life screwed her over.* The last thing she needed was for another one to do it again, even if it was her brother. Especially her drunk brother. All the men back when Mary still dated were drunks. Mean ones, not like Brown. Not a drunk like him who wouldn't touch a hair on a person's head. These boys did more than touch hairs on Mary's head, they ripped some of them out.

Brown took his drink somewhere else to enjoy the buzz alone. Their mother used to find him drinking under the porch, in the basement, up in the woods, in the bored-out space behind the train tunnel with tar dripping all around. *A real sight*, she'd say. It was in the hideout not a quarter of a mile from the high school where he became a full-time drunk at the age of seventeen. His mom had almost ten years on Brown before she made it to that drowned out place, where a drink was the only thing a person wanted to hold anywhere near their heart. That place that left an emptiness so dark and so deep it hurt so bad a person stopped talking about it all together after a while—couldn't know how to make any sense of it out loud. But years passed and the hideout crumbled in on itself and filled up with the rain smells and the train sounds trapped inside.

Staying away from the drinking busted Brown daily. Not a week went by that there wasn't more days consumed by it than not. He'd wake up after a night drinking and promise himself and the sky, his sister and his mother's soul, that he would not touch a drink again. By that afternoon, there he'd be sitting on the train tracks down by Estill's body shop and garage drinking and talking to Estill. After that, he'd wander around until he passed out, most of the time around the apartment somewhere, but sometimes as far away as Beefhide or Jonancy. The first few times it was a major thing. Mary yelled at him for hours, read scripture and cried a little while Brown nodded off on the couch. She did all of this with a baby punching away in her gut at two in the morning. This baby grew up inside Mary hearing all of this on the inside, the yelling and the scripture, and with Mary still poor as a snake in her arms and legs, skinny as a rail, just a little baby belly. They thought the baby might be marked from it all when he was born, but that didn't happen. His daddy was off in the head, something even people who didn't say things like that said about him. But not a thing about that guy was normal. He didn't drink. He mashed up pills and then took it right up his nose, and got mean as a timber rattler after that. Mary wouldn't even mention his name. "Those not spoken of…" she said. But that baby got through it just fine. *Normal as anything.* Nicholas Clayton Taylor, the son, the nephew, and Brown didn't backslide again for almost a year after the boy kicked his way into this world.

The year Brown went sober, he spent a lot of time playing with Nick. At first he just cooed on the floor on thin blankets so the hardwood bit through into his ribs while Nick pounded him with balled up fists, slobbered all over his arms, chewing good and constant, trying to get his teeth to bust through his gums. After a while, Brown held his hands up, his fingers wrapped tight as belt buckles around Nick's thumbs, helping him take steps. It was a week before the first birthday party when Brown fell hard and got on a roaring drunk at Don Bentley's house. Mary wouldn't let him fool much with Nick after that, not for a while.

When Nick got older and was about to start school, Brown convinced her Nick needed some guidance in case anybody messed with him. He was talking by then and all he kept asking, while Brown tried to show him how to tuck a hard elbow into a kid's throat, was why everybody called him Brown Bottle.

Mary tried to kill him stone dead with a look.

"People are just crazy," Brown told him. "They make up names. That's what people do. Don't pay it a bit of mind."

Nick told him his breath smelled like poop and put a thin elbow into his collarbone.

Mary raised Nick to be Christian. Kept the drinking away. Told Brown to mouthwash, to keep it out of the house, the whole nine yards.

Gave him some options. *Hide a bottle at the dumpster and take the garbage out eight times a day. Stay over at Don's if you get under it. Do whatever you have to do, but keep it away from Nick.* He did absolutely as Mary said, for the most part. When he failed, he failed in large ways but not often. He'd never get forgiveness for breaking their daddy's plate brought from Cincinnati when he moved to Kentucky. That ugly plate somehow got to be like a magical totem or something like that after their Daddy died. Brown busted it against the wall one night while arguing with Mary about a Bill Withers song when really all that was in his mind was how much he hated their daddy, hate in his gut and his blood and his heart. So much so he could barely stand up with the weight of it.

It was no secret Brown thought the absolute world of Mary, strong as she was yet never taking the first sip of anything, even with their mother drinking around them day and night. *Lucky and brave and strong little sister.* It was well known he didn't even like insects to bite her. That's how personal he took it. And as sure as anybody knew this about Brown they knew he thought the same of Nick. That's why it was important for Brown to show him a few jabs and elbows before he started school. People in town knew them, knew their story just like Brown and Mary knew all the stories that made up all the people in town. It was that way in small towns. People could be mean and say things.

But Nick was to be raised Christian and that made learning hand-to-hand combat maneuvers tricky. Self-defense didn't fit into Mary's plans all that well. But she knew the world was mean, cruel and hard, so she left it alone. As was her custom in all things, she made one demand. She didn't want to see Nick coming at Brown with sweep kicks and throat gouges, so the two stayed at the east end of the field, away from the house. The field got to be like some kind of heaven to Brown. No screaming, no fighting. None of this, outside of him or inside of him. In the field with Nick, Brown went hours without a drop of anything, not even missing the smell. If he could've stayed in the field forever, hand to hand, learning how to keep the world from swallowing them up, he might have had a better chance at being a good Christian.

It was something like a poem seeing Nick trying so hard. Tiny little guy, red-brown hair like that old bastard who sweated over top of his mom and then split out fast, swinging away at Brown, and Brown taking those little punches right on the chin and across the cheek, letting him get the feel of his knuckles connecting. *It can be an odd thing, knuckles against bone, if you're not used to it*, Brown told him. He wanted Nick tough, but it was hard with Mary making sure he included as many bible stories as possible while instructing.

So there he would be, explaining the best way to hyperextend a kneecap while telling about David bringing down old Goliath and how that fight was worth something. *Only fight when it's worth something*, he told Nick. People thought fighting was about being cool, but Brown always told Nick, *That's a bunch of bull poop. David fought for his life, and that was the best thing to ever fight for, ever.*

Most of the summer they stayed out in the field, but it wasn't all combat training for kindergarten. Sometimes the two of them sat at the end of the creek and tossed rocks, and Nick would call him Brown Bottle trying to get him worked up and Brown would pretend to get mad, charge full steam and then let Nick trip him into the grass, let him see all the work was paying off, that the hours spent out in the summer sun in the field with his crazy old uncle had taught him a thing or two. The last week before kindergarten classes started, though, it was a foxhole Nick wanted Brown to make. Instead of digging a ditch across the field, Brown, with Nick's helping a little here and there, dug a square out seven feet by seven feet and then trenched it out another seven feet. They found two large sections of wood paneling and fixed them together and covered the hole. That last week the two of them stayed in the foxhole more than they stayed outside or in the house.

When he got on the school bus the first morning, Brown saw the fight in his eye, saw it planted there, firm and solid. He waved at the bus driver and then took a seat wherever he wanted. He seemed confident and ready. Mary cried after the bus left. Brown's hand went easy to her shoulder. Without looking at him she said he smelled like a brewery.

Days lasted too long for Brown through the week when Nick was away at school. After that first week, he told Brown that he hadn't used a single thing that they worked on in the field. Brown began staying in the field all through the day. A bruised-up tin bucket sat at the far corner of the field where he kept some vodka. Without a second thought, he'd drink from one side of the clock to the other, the field stretched out all around him like one of those thin blankets on the hardwood floor of the world. And Brown didn't make a dent in it. Meshed together with the earth like that, he was as small as any other blade of grass. He told himself bible stories then. Ecclesiastes. *To everything there is a season, and a time to every purpose under heaven. Up and down in the field all day.* That's what he did. Praying hard for an elbow to the throat.

1

It was an odd thing for Mary to walk away from her only child. And the way she did it had even people who didn't usually talk about them talking about them all around town. Brown heard it outside the library while he sat in the shade of his favorite tree during his favorite time of day for shade. *These two little ladies, these sweet looking ladies, talking about Mary Taylor and how she left her boy to live with that drunk. Probably end up a drunk, too. Probably already a drunk. Probably why she left. But still, the way she did like that. That woman.* Behind the high school gym where the river was always the quietest, he overhead the head coach of the boys' basketball team and his assistant coach talking over a shared cigarette. *That Mary Taylor was still a hot one. I wouldn't kick her out of bed in the dark, maybe. Just a one-night thing, though, because that bitch has a heart of pure cold. Real ice cold kind of shit. Hot, though, for a whore and an older woman. Have to give her that.*

The talk did more than upset Brown. It made him see red. He wanted to rip their skin off, even the sweet-looking ladies at the library, but especially the coach and his guy out back of the gym. And that it often times included terrible remarks about Nick was worse. *Nick didn't deserve a single word of it. Mary, though, Mary didn't deserve most of it, either.* Some of it Brown couldn't argue with. She had dropped everything, left for another town, another life. That Mary had simply never been one for giving up was the strangest thing of all. Those long days when she and Brown were younger and stayed tired all the time from working around the house and keeping up the outside of the house so there'd be no beatings or fights, Mary was always there with her head held in the air, always a little piece of granite complaining because Brown forever tried finding ways to get out of chores. Even then he seemed to prefer punishment to honest work. The drinking had already started and Mary soon could only see it as a weakness in both character and spirit.

But then and now there wasn't a soul who would call what he and Mary had to do actual chores. It was more than that. Their father hated them for breathing, and their mother stayed too drunk to care. It was a bad country song, but it was true all the same. The one time their mother said much about it at all she took Mary aside on the front porch. Brown had a washtub playing with it in the yard and could hear the two of them talking in low whispers. He heard her tell Mary that their cruel father, the hateful man lording over all of them, had wanted both of them aborted. Sweet Mary asked what aborted meant and their mother was saying very slowly the word *murdered.*

Hearing this made Mary stronger and harder. She defied their father every chance she got, would laugh when he hit her whenever she was able. Once, he punched her mouth and it instantly filled with blood. She spat it back at him. She was ten and Brown was eight. But for every bit of courage Mary stored up, Brown lost more and more. He stole more of their mother's beer and, later on, found the places she stashed liquor and moonshine. Most of the time he was caught drinking and their father beat him without mercy. But it was hardly more than a dull thumping inside his skull. The alcohol protected him, kept him from feeling the pain.

While Brown drank, Mary grew up nicely, shapely, and boys noticed, as boys will. It didn't matter to any of them that Mary might as well have been a nun, married to Christ and entirely faithful. They came anyway. They knocked on the front door and when Rachel told them her daughter was gone, died, in the shower, moved away, and many other excuses, they came back at night to knock on windows until they found her bedroom.

Mary eventually gave in at the age of sixteen to a boy named Eddie Joe Maynard. By this time, their father had already left. His standing threat to kill any boy found around his place had vanished with him to Eleven County where he worked as a roving mine electrician. Eddie Joe had been the most persistent and also could not have been more different than Mary. He drank with Brown at the beginning, giving Mary little mind while the two of them sat by the creek bank and finished off bottles of cheap vodka and whiskey. Eddie Joe would buy the stuff from Stab, a truck driver and part time bootlegger. Sometimes it was a good bottle of Jim Beam and other times it was hard moonshine in the tiny water bottles they kept around coal mines for miners to hydrate their dusty throats. He brought moonshine the day Mary finally gave him some attention.

She called out his name, and Eddie Joe left Brown sitting on the creek bank with four bottles from the six he'd brought. Two things happened in the next hour, Mary lost her virginity to Eddie Joe and Brown made his first trip to the hospital to have his stomach pumped. Alcohol poisoning hit him after downing four bottles of prime moonshine within half an hour.

It wasn't something Brown could really make out in words, but he understood how the two events were significant and married to one another in some kind of tragedy. His drinking and the beginnings of Mary's troubles with men. It was four months before Brown drank another drop and four months before the first large bruise appeared under Mary's eye. Others followed and then cuts across her forehead or patches of her hair pulled loose all at once so that you could see the burr of her hair lying bloody against her scalp. Brown drank instead of facing Eddie Joe and then, sober the next day, punched the walls at the studs until his knuckles bled.

When Mary walked out one morning from her bedroom with her bottom lip split so severely it mostly hung from her bottom row of teeth, Brown tried to blind-side Eddie Joe at Stab's house. He punched the older boy in the back of the neck, but he might as well have patted him for the all the damage it caused. Eddie Joe whipped him flat to the ground while Stab watched with a grin, sipping Jim Beam and Coca-Cola from a plastic cup, rooting for Eddie Joe the same way someone might cheer on a baseball team.

It was red cherry whiskey Brown wanted while in the library asking questions about how to get on the internet. He'd tried calling the places Mary had mentioned in the two letters he'd gotten, he'd tried directories, Mary's friends, all the normal means of communication. Now he sat in the Estelle Marie Bell Memorial Library talking to a woman with a squat way of standing directly over his shoulder about reverse searches and whether or not he knew Mary's G-mail address.

"Her what?"

"Her G-mail," the woman said. The library was otherwise empty. Seemingly bored, the librarian had taken a special interest in his quest to reach his sister with bad news. "Her email address. It's pretty much like what letters used to be except a billion times faster and better. You probably don't have a G-mail, but we can fix you up. It's fast and easy. Does your sister have one?"

Brown looked over his shoulder at the girl. She smiled, had her arms crossed behind her back and leaned forward just like he pictured people would when skiing.

"I've got an address."

"A physical address?"

"What the heck other kind would it be?" Brown asked.

"I mean the address where she's living at now," the librarian said.

"It's on the envelope."

He knew Mary was at their uncle's house in Ohio. Chillicothe, Ohio. They kept old phone numbers somewhere. Mary always stored things like that, phone numbers, recipes, letters, poems she had written while growing up. Bits and pieces of family and memories of some kind of goodness and maybe something to remind her they weren't alone. But even though she feared being alone, the day he left for the military her smile just went on and on, stretched across her whole face. He went blackout drunk the first chance he had during basic training and then forgot how much Mary seemed to hate him, how she could turn hatred on him when that's all they ever got from anybody.

He was nearly dishonorably discharged that fast, but it had been Rusty who wrote on his behalf and persuaded them differently. Rusty had served and knew what to say and how to say it. He had been drafted, not a volunteer. But after another couple weeks, Brown leveled out, got comfortable with his station and his duties. It turned out he was suited for the whole thing. Some would say they wouldn't find that at all surprising, but they wouldn't really understand at all what they were talking about.

Brown watched the librarian walk back to the front counter where the new bestsellers were arranged. She had a nice figure for a middle-age woman, a sweet voice. A really nice smile. What they said about most of the men in Sandy was that once a woman left her twenties, they became suddenly less interested. And that was true for most of them, but Brown was not among them. In fact, he often visited the library just to see her.

Blair. That was her name. And he wasn't so sure he ever wanted to know her last name. *Blair.* He came at least once a week and rented a few VCR tapes and the VCR to go with it. She always smiled and told him he was the only person in the last twenty years to check out the VCR or any movies for it. She told him they kept them around just for him. Each time he made his returns, she asked about the movies. Was *Rocky II* as good as the first one? Which of the *Back to the Future* movies was his favorite? She seemed genuinely interested and uncaring whether or not he was drunk. If she was making fun of him, Brown was having a hard time noticing.

"Bring that address back in and I'll find what you need in no time at all." She smiled and was shocked when Brown quickly stood up and walked at a fast pace out of the library.

He dialed the number carefully, after each digit glancing back at the thin paper he found inside the family bible. It was an Ohio prefix. Their uncle's house. Their mother's older brother, a welder and another in a long line of drunks. He picked up on the fourth ring.

"I thought people hung up after three rings," Brown said and tried a light chuckle that came out sounding fake and nervous.

"Hi, Rusty. It's Wade, Rachel's boy."

"Looking for her I figure."

"You'd figure right," Brown answered. "You remember her little boy, Nick, don't you?"

There was silence at the other end.

"Well, he's going downhill and fast" Brown continued. "Drugs, trouble, stealing, staying gone from home for weeks at a time, fighting. You name it. No jail time yet, but it's coming. Won't be long."

"What kind of drugs?" Rusty asked. "I mean if he's having a joint now and then, what's the big deal?"

"Oxycontin," Brown said.

"Oh, okay, yeah that's some bit worse. That's the hillbilly heroin, right?"

Brown knew he was talking about meth, but didn't correct him. "Well, it's bad enough. It's for cancer patients, dying cancer patients, Rusty. I swear I think he's crunching it all up and sniffing it up his nose. And he's stealing so he can buy more and more."

"Like cocaine back in the seventies. Snorting it," Rusty said.

"What? I don't know, I guess so. He's stealing, Uncle Russ, that's what I'm saying, and using really bad drugs. Mary needs to know, that's why I'm calling."

"Haven't seen her in years, bub," he said. "Probably since the last time I saw you."

He could hear the lie in Rusty's voice. It was a talent cultivated over the years while protecting himself from harm. Most often someone lying to him was the rainclouds and the hurting was the storm that followed, thunder and all, lightning, the crying of hounds in the dark, the scrambling of birds from treetops.

"She's there, Rusty. I know she is, just tell her to come to the phone."

"Sonofabitch, Wade, I done told you she ain't here."

Brown heard Rusty's voice trail off fast and then a rattling somewhere hundreds of miles away, an echo of footsteps, and finally Mary's voice at the other end.

"Wade, I don't have time for this. I have a double to pull starting at three this afternoon." Her voice wasn't tired, Brown thought. She sounded cheery. "Russ says it's about Nick. Well, I've done all I can for Nick. He's grown now."

He pictured her standing with the phone at her ear. She wore a uniform, probably a waitress outfit. Rusty behind her with his arms crossed. He was always a pervert. Their mother's youngest brother, now an old man harboring a niece wanting to escape from the world she once knew, and willing to do so if only for the chance to see her wrapped in a bath towel or sleeping in her panties and bra on a night too muggy for blankets. Rusty would be staring at her, looking her up and down. But he was the only uncle the two of them had, and so Mary went to him when she wanted to better herself in a different place, and now Brown was on the phone with him for about the same kind of reason. But still, he could picture his uncle with a hateful look on his face, stealing glances at Mary's bra strap. He pictured Mary laughing with her mouth covered.

"I love you, Mary, but I don't understand how you can just throw down your family like you're doing," Brown said. "Nick's using drugs and stealing. How'm I supposed to do anything with him?"

Her voice came fast into the receiver. "I didn't just throw down *nothing*, Wade. I fought and fought to make what little was there some kind of family. All you did was drink and piss yourself and whine.

You never did *nothing*. You think 'cause you took an interest in Nick and hung out with him some that makes you something special? You are badly fooled. You think that makes you special and me some kind of monster now that I'm going on with my life and leaving Nick to his? You are badly fooled."

Brown let that set in the air and leveled out his breathing. He looked around his shoulder to see if Mrs. Hudson still stood behind him watching to make sure he didn't go over five minutes on his long-distance call, but she was gone.

"I'm on Mrs. Hudson's phone here, Mary, so I don't have but about two more minutes or so. I guess I just wanted you to know what all was going on, but I could sure use some advice or something. I know you don't want Nick ending up like all these other kids around here, at the morgue or in the jailhouse."

He could hear Mrs. Hudson shuffling through the hallway, the tinkling of the whatnot shelf as she grabbed hold for better purchase meant his call was about to end no matter the two minutes he had left.

"I know what I have to do, Mary," he said. "I'm not talking about me right now, I'm talking about you and about how you need to be here for Nick."

"I got to get to work, Wade. I'm not throwing nobody down, but you do what you think you need to do." She paused and Brown could hear keys rattling. "But you're not going to get far drunk as a dog and still whining to me. Nick knows I'm here at Rusty's. If he needs me, he'll come to me. And I won't send him packing. But until then, he's got his life to live and I've got mine. Live yours, why don't you. Sober up. Help your nephew if that's what you want to do, but sober up. He ain't going to listen to a word you say if you're standing drunk in front of him."

She hung up just as Mrs. Hudson made her way to the phone base and pressed a birdbone thin finger on the button to end the call.

"Time's up," she said. She held out her hand. Her eyes were clear, a bright blue, her mouth tight, expecting exactly what it asked for.

Brown blew air between his teeth before he could catch himself and Mrs. Hudson's eyes grew wide. She pushed her hand out closer to his chest. He fished around in his pocket and found the ten he was saving for a bottle of Tvarski, dropped it in her hand.

"That should've probably bought me more than five minutes."

"Well, get you about ten or so more of those and you can hook up a phone of your own and you won't have to be standing around in my kitchen all the time. Good day to you, Brown. Good day."

She began sweeping him toward the front door. Brown thanked her and was digging in his back pockets just in case he overlooked a couple dollars when she closed the door behind him.

2

The town of Sandy was never truly quiet. There was a buzz, something electric going all the time. Streetlights, a piece of machinery at the truck garage across from the gas station, a low hum that seemed to come off the pavement, like the sun had pressed hard into it during the day and the heat sizzled up to the surface to join all that low sound. Sometimes it was hardly more than an occasional rattle from a Pepsi machine at the corner of the American Electric Power building.

Brown stopped at the pop machine and checked it for change. *One dime.* He palmed it and looked the ground over for any that may have been dropped in a rush. He tried to think of anyone he hadn't borrowed money from around town, but he'd covered about the whole place in the past week alone. He didn't want to do it, but he'd have to go by Janice's Sweet Tooth if he wanted a drink.

Janice Engle owned the only shop in Sandy that wasn't a farm and garden place or a gas station. She was already wealthy when she opened it, which Brown was sure had to be the reason it hadn't closed. Janice painted the front door pink the first day the lease was signed. Brown opened the pink door and walked inside.

The whole place smelled like cake and icing. The walls had shelves, and on the shelves were fresh made cupcakes, sour straws, white chocolate brownies, slices of cherry delight. Janice stood at the counter. When she looked up and saw Brown, she took off her glasses and sat down a book she had been reading.

"How's your constitution, Wade?"

Janice always called him Wade. She was a good woman, even for a rich lady, what folks still called a spinster around Port County. A shade or so past her fifties without having married. No kids. But she would have been a great mother, Brown always said. Except for spoiling kids with sweets. That would be the only downfall Brown could figure, and that wasn't much compared to some others. Though Janice was only ten years older than he, Brown had imagined what it would be like if she were his mother.

Brown nodded and sat down at one of the front counter stools. Sometimes it was like this, Brown stopping by and not saying much. There were times when he had to have time to sit in a room with someone like Janice.

"I'm helping Wilson down there at the pool, covering it for winter," Brown said. "He asked me to come up here, and he ain't got hold of me in a few days."

"Might be he's taking a brief break and just hasn't managed to get hold of you to tell," Janice said.

"I don't know. Maybe."

Brown sat at the small bar along the left side of the shop, the one with the window looking out onto Route 122. Janice came from behind the counter, took care to adjust a stool next to him and sat down. The two of them sat looking out the window.

"You still getting some business?" Brown asked finally.

"Not very often," Janice said. She wiped something invisible from the front of her apron and smiled while looking out the window. "But that's perfectly fine with me. I didn't open this place to make money."

Janice had these odd thoughts out loud a lot. It was another reason Brown liked to stop by. Janice thought about things differently than other people in Port County. It helped to see that such a thing was possible.

"You just like making cakes for folks?"

Janice laughed. She laughed with her whole face, her mouth spreading out to show straight, white teeth. Her blue eyes seemed to catch every bit of light in the shop. "Well, it's not something I have a problem doing, but I'll tell you the real reason I started this, if you promise to keep it between just you and I, Wade."

Brown nodded.

"You remember my father, don't you?"

"Sure."

"When he became severely ill, when the hospital sent him home to more or less die, no one in the family wanted anything to do with that problem," she said. "This was well before the concept of hospice or anything like that, so someone had to take care of him. I was that someone. I started this shop to get away from that day-to-day, well, the horror of it all."

She moved back behind the counter and took a deep breath. "I made this shop as a place to get away from the reality of watching him die. Soon as I had his breakfast prepared and fed to him, I came here. With the old homeplace only a short walk away, I could check in on him without having to *be* there all the time. I'm not proud of that, but it's the truth."

"You had a burden on you, the taking care of him," Brown said. "I know that feeling, believe you me."

Janice smiled again. She picked up a *People* magazine and adjusted her glasses on her nose.

"I guess I'll be heading out," Brown said. "I don't know what I'm going to do about Wilson with that pool job. He must not have much trouble paying his power bill if he's able to wait off work like that."

Janice sat her magazine down and took a ten dollar bill from the register. She handed it to Brown. "Go on, Wade. Get a cupcake on your way out."

Brown nodded and felt gratitude swelling up in his stomach and into his chest. He didn't know where Judy learned to treat people the way she did, but he was glad for it. Her daddy was a good man, people said. Brown never met him, but he was a carpenter, and somehow that always seemed like a good thing to be. Judy must have taken after him, some of that ability to see past a problem or a person's flaws to their potential and be decent to them.

"Wilson will get in touch soon, I'm sure," she said.

"I sure hope so."

He left the shop eating a strawberry cupcake.

Brown walked the first hill on High Street and turned left up a banked driveway to Van Hall's body shop. Van stood outside watching a boy swing a Weedeater along a hillside that dove off sharply from his main garage. Brown recognized the boy from around here and there but wasn't sure of his name. He knew he was from the Jonancy line of Stewarts and that line of Jonancy residents were trouble. Most or all were in and out of jail most of the time, or drunks, pill heads, thieves, high school dropouts, welfare frauds. He was Brown's kind of people. The kind everybody else hated. Van's son Doug was another one of that kind. He was Brown's best friend.

Van noticed Brown on the hill and walked inside his main office, a sectioned off area of the bay garage that had a small television, some snack cakes for sale, and a few car parts scattered around collecting dust. It was said Van still had the first dollar he ever made. Two homes, countless vehicles, a cabin in Tennessee, a houseboat. Those were the only ways you'd ever know he had money at all. He used both of his boys to work the body shop for years and years. Brown used to visit and find himself stripping the decal off the hood of a T-Bird or masking off a section of a bumper, or sandwashing some other car before anything else could be done. But Brown had never known Van to work for anybody but himself, and that was sure something. It wasn't everybody could say that around eastern Kentucky, where you couldn't sneeze without having to apologize to a coal miner. And the coal mine answered to suits in Frankfort who answered to suits in Washington. When Brown walked in, Van slumped deeper into in his recliner and turned the television up.

"Hiya, Van."

Van wore the same clothes most every day. A short-sleeve blue Dickies work shirt, darker blue Dickies work pants, and a pair of cheap maroon running shoes, the kind with Velcro straps instead of shoestrings. There was always a brief banter between the two. Brown felt generally obliged to say a few words, when all he ever wanted to know was where Doug had got off to.

"Some of us got to work for a living," Van said. He didn't look away from the television.

So it was going to be another short exchange with Van mostly insulting him in a roundabout sort of way as usual.

"Where abouts is Doug today?"

"I'll be damned if he ain't working to make a living, too. Can you believe that shit?"

Brown didn't say anything. It was always like this, Van casting insults and then smiling as if the smiling made up for it, somehow made it perfectly fine to put down another man who had done nothing to wrong him, who had never so much as looked sideways at him.

Van finally turned down the set.

"He's working up at Bob Allen's number four mine at Carbon Glow," he said. "He says he's an outside man, but he's mostly just a glorified night watchman. I doubt he even charges scoops."

"I know the place. Right there above the Carbon Park, right?"

"You got it."

A snapping from outside distracted Van, and he jumped up, arms swinging, and disappeared around the corner of the garage. Brown could hear Van laying full blast into the boy cutting grass for busting the head on the Weedeater. The kid would have to buy another head to replace the busted one on credit and that would mean half the pay. There wasn't a sound from the boy. Brown started walking toward Carbon Glow.

Two drivers familiar with him gave him a lift, and so Brown made it to Carbon Park within the hour, just before October dark craned like a folding wing over the hollow. It was a short walk to the mine, a trench cut away along the ridgeline and into the body of the mountain with a large enough seat for one full garage, the mine face, and an area for the trucks to park for loading. A shortbed was parked nearly beneath the belt drop where a thin line of coal moved and fell onto not a very large pile. Seemed Bob Allen had almost mined this vein out.

At the top of the small hill Brown stopped at the guard shack. Music pounded from inside. *Guns N' Roses. Classic.*

Brown twisted the cap from the pint of whiskey he bought at Bill C's. After Man Dodge picked him up hitching, he was kind enough to stop at Bill C's for him, understood what it was like to need a drink. He hadn't thought to open it until standing outside the guard shack listening to Axl Rose hit the high notes. Not exactly his type of music, but he always thought it was the closest thing to rock and roll since early Rolling Stones. Lifting the bottle to his nose, he inhaled deeply, coughed, and spun the lid back on. He gave three fast knocks on the flimsy screen door and heard a series of shuffles before the music cut off abruptly.

Doug pulled the door open. Brown could see right away he'd been asleep.

"What if I'd been Bob Allen stopping to check up?" Brown said and gave him a light punch in his pot belly.

Doug had looked to be in about his mid-thirties since they were in high school. Went bald early, had the ever present paunch, early pockmarks from acne. And, aside from the fact that he had taken more illegal substances than any of the Oxyheads in the Big Sandy Region combined, he was the most confident, most charismatic, and most loyal person Brown knew.

"Christ almighty, man. Thought you were the guys inside coming back to bitch about me turning the extraction fan on backwards."

"Backwards?"

"Yeah, however you say it. Backwards, reversed. I turned the fan on when they called out for it, and it was blowing air into the mine instead of pulling it out," he said. "Backwards. Folks almost died. People were pissed. Not fired, though, so there's that at least."

Doug turned a floor heater off, and the shack was at once too quiet.

"Turn Guns back on and grab us a couple chairs," Brown said.

Doug came back out with two metal folding chairs and a couple Tall Boy cans of Budweiser. He motioned to a makeshift walkway that ran above the belt line and started walking. Brown followed, listening to the opening of "November Rain" build and watching coal trickle out from the mountain in one thin line before falling over the end of the belt in a gray-black swoosh. Doug stopped before going up to the steps to the walkway, eyed the line.

"Hang on," he said.

He took a piece of yellow chalk from the back of his pocket and jogged a few yards toward the drop, turned, and made a slashing yellow mark on the belt.

"Another tear," he explained. "That belt is just one big tear. I mark it and they go right on like everything's just fine, and the belt breaks and there goes hours of work and loss of coal." He took a long swallow of his beer.

"Can't see what it really matters to you, Douglas," Brown said.

"Well, it don't much, except if this one closes or gets red tagged then I'm out of a job and you know where that puts me, right?"

"Back in the garage with the old man. Got it."

The two of them sat quietly for a time, arms draped over the walkways single rail. The backside was only cut mountain. Once it was fully dark, Doug got up saying he had to toss some coal to the split barrel fire. Brown watched him step up to the belt and grab two soccer ball sized chunks and place them at his feet. He looked back up at the belt and waited with his hand hovering and grabbed a large flat slate rock from the belt, looked at Brown and nodded as if to say, *Look at the shit-rocks this mountain is handing out today.* He picked the two good chunks up and tucked them under his arms and disappeared into the main building.

With Doug inside, Brown took the pint in hands again, eyed the Tall Boy unopened between his feet. The last time he sat with Doug at a mine night watching they both woke the next morning convinced they had seen a cigar-shaped UFO during the night. This was on Little Robinson Creek a few years back, the peak of his blackout era and also Doug's worse time with meth. So there may have been a UFO spying on a drunk and a meth head at two in the morning that night or, just as possible, they both may have been simply wiped off their asses and higher than Georgia pines. That night started exactly as this night was starting.

Brown again spun the cap back on the pint, but sat it beside his beer this time instead of pocketing it. Doug came back out turning up his own beer in a drain and then tossed the can onto the belt where it rode like a silver coin off the end of the belt and into the dark forever of tons of blackness.

"Scoops are good, the fire's stoked, and the fan is not the death machine it once was," Doug said when he sat back down. "All we have now are the hours."

It was like that sometimes, Doug being poetic. He could surprise a guy.

"I'm going to have to try to stop drinking," Brown said quickly.

Doug didn't respond, not really. He sniffed and smiled, picked up the pint at Brown's feet, opened it, and took a decent pull.

"Now why's that?"

"So I can focus on helping Nick. Buddy, he's into bad, Doug. I mean about the worse bad you've seen. Maybe not bad as you've been, but bad enough. Oxys and stealing and all that. You know the song."

"He snorting Oxys or just doing them regular?"

Brown didn't know, and surely didn't know what Doug meant by regular.

"I think he's snorting some," he finally said. "Like crushing a bunch up and sniffing them up. Cocaine. Like that."

"Shit that is bad, Wade, but it still don't mean he's into real bad, not exactly. I knew this guy one time." He stopped and looked at Brown. "And I mean I really just knew this guy. I wasn't this guy. I just knew him. But I knew this guy one time, he was so far gone he used to take his girl with him to his dealer to get pills and let the dealer have sex with her for their fix. Both of them were pill heads. So this dealer, he gets all creative and the next time the two of them show up, you know what he says, man?"

"I kind of don't want to," Brown answered.

"I kind of don't want to even think about it either, but this dealer, he tells the guy that he can have his usual weeks' worth for free if he lets him, you know, gouge the girlfriend right there in front of him."

"Whose girlfriend?"

"The pill head's girl. The dealer, see, just wanted to know how far this poor guy would go, how much of his pride he'd piss away for just a handful of pills."

Brown felt punched in the side of the head. "So what happened?"

"He did it. I mean he did it all the way."

"How in the world would anybody even hear about something like that?" Brown said. Saying it made the pain in his head ease up, helped his stomach settle.

"Look here, my man, I wish it wasn't true, too. But it is. My cousin told me." Doug twisted open Brown's whiskey and took a short pull before continuing. "He's a probation and parole officer, and this guy was one of the people on his client list. He let me read the report where the guy had to detail all of it for pretrial."

Brown let out a long breath and took the bottle from Doug. He used to chase whiskey with Mountain Dew. Not because he couldn't take the taste and needed it diluted, but because he liked the way the two tasted together. He didn't miss his can of Mountain Dew. He didn't miss the sting of the whiskey on his tongue, his throat, and then the nice warm spread in his stomach. In fact, his stomach turned over and over as he watched the line of coal moving below him like a spear of dark flood water. He kept seeing the girlfriend's face while she bent over for the dealer, the pill head's face, kept thinking of where their hearts must have been at that moment, where it must have hidden inside them, muted and split in two. Just as Doug reached for the bottle again, Brown dropped it onto the beltline. It clicked against the coal and then sped away from them like a silverfish.

Doug said, "What in the holy hell?"

"I reckon I'm going to have to be done with the drinking," Brown said. "Reckon I can't help Nick unless I do. He *cannot* end up like this feller you're talking about. Lord in heaven, he cannot."

Doug looked off into the distance. "It's okay, I've got a few beers left in there."

"Well, alright, then, brother," Brown said, slapping Doug on the leg and pulling himself up from the chair. "I'm out of here."

Doug didn't say anything while he walked away from the mine face, but when Brown turned around just before heading back down the hill to the two-lane road, Doug put his hands up to his mouth.

"Could've gave me the whiskey!"

Brown waved his arm but kept his eyes on the road while yelling back to Doug. "Thought about that, but it was too late."

3

At the end of Garden Road stood a garage. A block building with a set of double wooden doors swinging out for cars or chairs, depending on whether work needed to be done or sitting and drinking and getting high needed to be done. Sundays most of the work took place here, at the end of the road. Other days, the doors were closed, tight as a nun's knees. These days traffic sped down North Front Street that led to the garage and to the trailer beside the old structure, gravel and dirt tossed around like split barrel ash, a dark thing flying through clean air. Here folks from Port County to Teller County would swing in to meet with Tuck.

Tuck's brother, Stan, had been working on a 1998 Ford Ranger for more than four months at the garage, mostly Sundays, because the traffic to his brother's trailer was too much for him or anybody to handle, really. He'd yelled away a few buyers, but mostly just had to walk back the quarter mile to his house and leave it alone. His brother helped locals with needs, but all Stan wanted was to get that Ranger running. Younger brothers and giving in and allowances kept his progress at a slow gate, a shoulder-slumped walk across the bottom that crossed Garden Road and led to Stan's house across Route 122. From the front porch he could still keep an eye on the Ranger and how it tilted like a tired old man, the bumper at rest against the cherry picker.

"Stan! Phone!"

Stan shuffled his feet across the porch, his pant legs stuffed inside work boots. Grease coated the hard steel tips and sides. Once up, he stretched from habit and eased into the living room. His wife, a stick woman that he and everybody else called Hen, but whose real name was Henry because she had a strange daddy, held the phone out like a dead cat.

"Who's it?"

"Brown Bottle," she said. "Real good company you're keeping there."

Stan took the phone, pushed his boots off at the door and fell into the kitchen chair near the wall phone. He pulled the tangles out of the cord.

"Yeah?"

"Nick been coming over there to your brother's?"

He'd seen Nick Taylor come in and out a few times in the last few months. *Young boy with a broken mama and Wade for an uncle.* It made sense to Stan.

"I've seen him come by some. What can a person do? He's got a car now, Brown."

Stan waited with the phone hooked into his shoulder, putting bread in the toaster. A jar of apple butter in the middle of the table.

"Stan, I'd just as soon you call me Wade. He been out there buying?"

Stan closed his eyes then opened them. Hen watched from the doorway. She seemed punier than yesterday. Everything did.

"I'd figure so, yeah," Stan said. "Tuck don't run a card game, and he sure as shit don't have a book club."

The receiver went dead in his ear. Stan handed the phone back to Hen.

"That what I think it's about?" she asked. "That nephew of his? Nick?"

She moved though the kitchen, all skinny hips and legs, ivory arms bare from her pushed up sleeves weaving the air as she walked. She sat down at the table and opened the apple butter. Her hair was sunshine, Stan always said, even in the most swallowing darkness. She pushed the jar to Stan. Her eyes watched him, that caring affection she hid so well. But Stan could see worry there in her brow, a deep worry trying to hide itself away in all that blue. She pushed her hand across the table and he took it.

Stan didn't answer her question about Nick. He buttered a piece of toast and walked to the window. Four cars were in Tuck's driveway, best he could tell. Two more were parked out in the bottom where the old man and woman once farmed, a lot better than he and Tuck farmed it these days. That was mostly just enough corn to hide the pot growth, and a few patches here and there where they let neighbors grow small crops. A long stretch ran with the river's edge and the train tracks beyond. No sign of Nick's '78 Dodge Aspen. He'd have a look again in a half hour or so for Brown, walking up Garden Road. Until then, he'd check his shotgun, give it a good cleaning, make sure he had at least two shells left from last season. Man needed to be prepared.

The broken sounds of Stan sleeping on the couch put Hen in a restless mood. She made some calls to her folks, worked to fix the porch swing, fed the dogs. But she was still restless. At last, she sat in the recliner and watched her husband sleep. He was a tall man and his socked feet lopped over the end of the couch arm. His pants, two sizes too big, were rolled at the cuffs. Parts of his pallid shin were visible on one leg. The fall jacket she'd bought him two years ago was still zipped to the stubble of his double chin. He snorted, full and loudly, just as she was about to recall the jaw line of his youth. She turned on the television, then turned it off.

Vehicles kept filing in and out at Tuck's trailer, spilling every assortment of ragged men and women, some barely making it to the porch before banging shut the trailer door behind them. A couple mostly carrying each other to the door, dressed entirely in camo. Another group of three teenagers laughing while one stopped at the edge of the trailer to piss. One man in mining pants and shirt drove up in a state truck for mine inspectors and came back out carrying two medicine bottles, popping the top on one and swallowing down several pills before getting back in the cab. Each person stayed about ten minutes or so and then gravel and dust again and another crew.

Hen put on her windbreaker, left the living room, and sat on the swing, tested it for a few seconds, and then lit off down the porch steps. Crossing the bottom field she spotted two cars at one end of Tuck's then another when she rounded the corner to the porch. She knocked on the door and a stranger answered, shirtless and leaning. The stranger's stomach was large and tight and shined full and round in the sunlight.

"Ain't you a sight," she said. "Where's Tuck?"

The stranger smacked his lips and stepped back from the doorway. "Tuck!"

Hen flinched when the man yelled, but hid it well. She pulled her windbreaker around her and thrust her chin out. The stranger turned left into the dimness of the trailer and soon Tuck came through the living room.

Tuck had always been smaller made than Stan. Narrow shoulders, tiny hands and short fingers. Even as a young man his brown eyes were always watering like he'd been crying and his face never took hair well. What he had instead were four or five patches of hair that looked more like a cluster of bee stingers popping straight out from his cheeks. When he was standing in the doorway, he scratched at one of two receding hair lines.

"Hey, Hen. How's every little thing?"

"Stan's up there sleeping with a gun tucked under his arm," she said. "Think that's got anything to do with you? I'm just saying. Do you think?"

"What the hell? What's he doing that for?"

Hen straightened her back, tiptoed into Tuck's face. "Somebody's coming to see you soon. Probably more than just this guy that Stan's watching for."

"What guy?"

"Hush it!" She leaned back, looked away from Tuck and his hurt face, out across the bottom field. That field hadn't seen a tractor in twenty years, not for any real gardening. "You need to talk to your brother. I ain't waking him up."

Without giving Tuck time to answer, Hen popped down the three small steps of the porch and turned the corner of the trailer where she stopped to listen for Tuck to close his door. When he did, she sat on the metal tongue of the trailer, took a deep breath, and put her head in her hands. Stan seemed to sleep more now. Getting older, both of them.

They needed to slow down and had, to a good extent. This hopping around and getting in the middle of things with Brown Bottle Taylor was not slowing down at all, and she was going to tell Stan that in no uncertain words.

The doctors had already put Stan on cholesterol medicine and told him to eat heart healthy food. It sounded to Hen like they were trying in a discreet sort of way to get Stan prepared for when he had a heart attack, so that it wouldn't be so much of a surprise when it happened. Still, all she wanted was for him not to get worked up, surely not about Tuck and the drugs. Stan had separated himself from all that back when Tuck still offered homemade beer with tiny bags of weed taped to the bottom of the bottles. It was so much more than that now. Hen needed for Stan to turn the other way for a while, and that wasn't something he was used to doing. She stood, pulled her hair back out of her eyes and around the tops of her ears and walked back the way she came so that the bottom field stretched out in front of her, a flat track of land and history leading away.

"I told him."

"You what?" Stan tugged at the sleeve of his shirt.

"And I told him he needed to talk to you. That you two need to talk."

He tugged the other sleeve and paced the kitchen. Midday warmed the field and the front porch. The frost from the morning was gone now. Stan looked to Tuck's trailer and then across the way to the garage and his Ranger.

"It's warm enough now for me to get some work done on the truck without freezing my ass off," he said. "I'll deal with him at some point. Or he'll deal with me. Or Wade Taylor will."

Hen pulled him back into the kitchen as he was opening the door. Her fingers pushed into the muscles at the bend of his arm, her face a blank slab of wood. She pointed out the kitchen window.

A Dodge Aspen slid past the garage and kicked gravel as it maneuvered into a parked position. Nick Taylor stepped out wearing a camouflage jacket, sweat pants and a baseball cap eased just over the top of his brow.

"Sonofabitch."

Hen said nothing. Stan left the kitchen and returned with the shotgun. He knew Hen would pull at him again, and he'd let her stop him. The gun wasn't for Nick, after all. And when she did, he allowed her to take it. He pulled his jacket together and stepped onto the porch.

The Aspen's a pile of junk metal, he thought, walking across the field. Out of habit, he side-stepped around Lafe Hill's patch of garden. Stan plowed up a spot for it every spring, after the last frost. It was the only time the bottom felt like home again, really. The only sense of family left in the bottom field was Lafe's sprinkle of lettuce and greens, and the few other plots for some locals on Garden Road. Stan hardly counted his and Tuck's corn in such company, not when it was really nothing more than cover. Lafe and his wife picked about once a week, hunkered over without talking. Just picking and placing and then gone. The two of them were in better shape than the Aspen.

Nick Taylor's beat down Dodge was parked more or less sideways about four feet from Tuck's front porch. The motor ticked loudly. Stan tried to remember to mention that oil should be added or changed. That ticking sound was no good. Even the Taylors deserved some advice on cars from time to time. He sucked in a deep breath and knocked on the door. When Nick answered, Stan pointed back at the Aspen.

"You're gonna need to add some oil or have it changed," he said and watched the young man's eyes grow just a bit wider, pupils pinpoints. *Just a baby, really. Hardly one-fifty soaking wet after Thanksgiving dinner.* "Just tell Tuck I'm working on the Ranger if he needs me."

Stan had been trying to get a rebuilt motor dropped in the Ranger the past couple weeks. The hoist rocked above him while he pushed against the body of the motor. The thin, metal legs swayed and bent to breaking. Stan let a grunt gush out of him and stood back, took a chunk of cut wood and wedged it hard into a space just in front of the radiator. The truck rocked from his pushing, but nothing gave way. From the corner of his eye, he ignored the fact that Tuck and Nick stood on the front porch watching.

He dropped back into the plastic lawn chair at the mouth of the garage and rubbed his hands. The pressure had left dents in the palms of his hands, and he thought of Manny, the dog he and Tuck had when they were young. Hauling it out to the tree line beside the river at the far end of the field, he and Tuck both had those same kinds of dents afterwards. They had cradled the bloated Lab in a potato sack, each of them holding a wrung up end until it seemed that rough cloth was going to push straight on through the skin and hit bone from the weight. Tuck dropped his end three or four times and the scent of that bloat and death would come up at them and they'd gag and complain until the old man would yell in from the field and tell them to keep it moving.

Once to the tree line, both dropped the Lab, really a mixed breed mutt more than anything, and those dents from where the cloth had bitten into the skin were pink and deep on both their hands. Tuck forgot the shovel and voted to toss the dog over the embankment instead of going through all the burying, saying his hands hurt. What Stan thought about now, sitting in the plastic lawn chair and watching him talk shoulder to shoulder with Nick Taylor, was how he walked back that morning to get the shovel and had buried the old Lab himself. It got his ass out of the chair, and the motor was soon rocking again, shifting the Ranger around like a strong wind. He wore himself out and had just sat down for a second time when the corner of his eye watched Nick go back into his brother's trailer. Tuck stood for half a beat on the porch and then started over to Stan. When he was a few feet out, he stopped.

"So Wade Taylor gonna show up today, huh?" Tuck said. He looked back to his trailer and then again at Stan. "Hen said I should talk to you. Not sure she meant about that, but I figured as much. She's the one told me about Wade, and said you had your shotgun shelled up and ready earlier. There's some trouble coming you think."

"I think."

Stan opened the driver's door on the Ranger and took a seat, glanced at the wobbling hoist and then got out and shut the door easily. The latch went into place with hardly a sound. He backed away slowly. His eyes were glazed, mouth slack. "There's not much I can do about who comes here. They come or they don't. I know you don't agree, but it's the damn truth."

Having Tuck cuss at him didn't hit Stan's ear just right. "That boy over there ain't just started driving. He's sixteen and got a uncle that'll blow a hole through everything in the southern end of the county, including Garden Road. Most especially Garden Road."

Stan imagined Nick slanted on the couch in Tuck's living room or tilted against the wall in the kitchen. Wasn't a soul in the county didn't know how close Wade Taylor held his nephew to his torn heart. Wade came back from Michigan about a decade ago after two years working at a factory there. He showed up twenty pounds lighter and older in the face after he told folks two men mugged and beat him into the hospital. Few knew for sure, but Wade talked around town about how he got rolled for drug money up in Michigan and how druggies and dealers should burn. More than once Stan himself was in the diner when Wade would proclaim how more than half the county should probably burn.

Tuck shrugged it off when Stan reminded him, the same way he had disregarded it before. The same way he disregarded most everything since being hooked became being a supplier. *Blindfolded and high. Might as well be dead already.*

"Boy could be in there with his eyes rolled back in head or foaming at the mouth right now and you'd be in a world of shit," Stan said. He had started back on rocking the motor from side to side. He quit and took the piece of cut wood again and began wiggling it into a place for some leverage.

Before Tuck answered, a state cruiser pulled into the driveway. The driveway was a turnabout drive and troopers had been down and made a

U-turn a few times in the past couple of months but nothing else. Tuck turned and gave the cruiser a wave that seemed to say he didn't care if they wanted to turn in his driveway, he could care less, have a nice day. But instead of turning, the cruiser parked beside the Aspen. A state boy Tuck didn't recognize, a young man likely fresh from academy, stepped out, nodded, and went to the Aspen's license plate. He bent just a little, checked a small slip of paper in his hand. Adjusting his hat, he turned and started toward the garage.

"Hellfire," Tuck whispered.

"Gentlemen," the state boy said, and gave his hat a goofy tip. "This car belong to Nick Taylor?"

Stan sat back in the chair and stared harder than he might have at Tuck. The state boy kept his eyes on Tuck. Smiling, Tuck stood up and stretched, scratched his bald spot and sifted his fingers through the tufts along the sides of his head.

"I guess it must be, officer," Tuck said. "You need to see him? Showed up here out of the blue about a half hour ago. I can get him for you."

The trooper smiled fake and wide, all teeth and screw you. "I'll just have a look."

"Not without a warrant, officer," Tuck shot back evenly.

Stan stood up and walked to the trooper, stuck out his hand. "I'm Stan Hall, officer. This is my garage here and my old trap of a Ranger. I'll get the boy if you'd like."

Stan tried to hide that he was holding his breath.

The officer looked to the trailer and then back to Tuck, squinted his eyes, and then removed his hat. "I suppose there's no harm in going about it that way, guys. I've just got a few questions for him. Get him out here and I'll take care of the rest."

"Fine and good. Fine and good," Stan said. "Tuck, see if you can get anywhere on scotching the legs on that cherry picker and I'll be right back."

Tuck cocked his head to the right, the way a dog might when confused, snorted once and went to the front of the truck. Stan started to the trailer and the trooper followed behind him. He was worried the fresh state boy was going to follow him in anyway, but the boy stopped at the front of his cruiser and adjusted the butt of his service pistol just an inch or two then leaned against the fender.

The trailer had been nice once, an eighty-foot Clayton 1990 model. Inside there was plenty evidence of people living there, mostly in discarded food wrappers and general disarray. Two large recliners were placed in front of a new flat-screen television somehow situated on the paneled living room wall. Stan pinched his nose shut through the kitchen and found Nick in the first bedroom on the left down the long hallway.

The boy lay across a mattress on the floor. Beside him was a dinner plate with pill powder still stuck to sections, covering part of one petal from the design of hearts and roses. It was one of their mother's plates. *Many suppers off that plate and now this.* The thought of it ran over Stan and he charged the bed and shook the boy by the shoulders, his head whipping back and then forward, powder flying from his nostrils as he came to and opened his eyes.

Nick mumbled awake and Stan took no time trying to decipher any of it as it hardly mattered. He also felt no need to warn Nick Taylor that the leather backseat of a state cruiser would be the next thing he smelled once they made it back through the kitchen. He simply took him under the arms and lifted him to a standing position and made his way back through the trailer, stopping at the front door long enough to shake him some more so the boy could stand on his own.

The state boy was still leaning against the fender when Stan guided Nick onto the porch then came out himself, side-stepping around him and down the steps. Nick was wobbling in the weak sunlight, a limp version of Wade Taylor's nephew, confused and tired. The trooper moved toward the porch.

"That's private property there, officer." It was Tuck. He had at some point left the garage and stood behind the cruiser. "From the looks of it, he'll fall right on down to you if you stand just about where you are."

Stan hushed him with a glare and took the boy's elbow, asking the trooper to step back until he could make his way down. As soon as they were both on the ground, the trooper stepped close to Nick. He leaned in close and must have spotted the powder around the boy's nose because he spun him quickly and popped handcuffs from his belt in one fluid motion. Nick was arrested between gusts of fast wind, it happened so quickly. The trooper loaded him into the back of the cruiser without a word, tipped his round brim again in Stan's direction and left, easing out of the gravel driveway, slower than necessary.

Stan and Hen lived in the old homeplace. The rooms were few but large. Black and white photographs framed in ornate wood hung from the walls. Stan studied the photograph that was outside the bathroom of his parents. It was taken when corn still stood tall and tomatoes and lettuce made green and red the field. In the photograph it was easy to see the wind is blowing with the tree branches bent westward, his mother caught in mid-stride some five feet or so behind his father, staring away from the camera, and his father fully facing the camera. Stan leaned close and noticed again how his old man's mouth was twisted just enough to be able to tell he was saying something, his leather arm sweeping out as if telling whoever was taking the photograph to move along, get away, nothing to see here. His face was severe. His mother's face was regal, chin tilted, the look of a sharecropper hanging onto pride with every bit of energy she could muster.

Hen stepped behind him and placed a hand at his elbow. "I always liked that picture, Dip."

"Yeah. Me, too." He kept his eyes on the photograph.

"I see you got the shotgun again."

The over-under shotgun leaned against the wall in front of Stan. Two shells slept inside the chambers. He picked the gun up and, touching her more lightly than he had in years, walked slowly down the hall and into the kitchen. Scents of breakfast nearly pulled him out of the place he'd fallen since Nick Taylor had been arrested less than an hour ago, but it passed and he went to the window. From there he could see the turn off from Route 122 onto Garden Road and the entirety of that road until it ended at the block garage. There sat his pitiful Ranger still tilted from the weight of the immovable engine stuck half in and half out of its body.

Then he saw him. Brown Bottle, always walking instead of driving from always being hammered drunk, staggered down the incline of road. He had already turned onto Garden Road and moved faster than Stan would have expected. He didn't see a gun on him, but then he probably wouldn't. It'd be a pistol stuffed away in his pants or in the armpit of his jacket. It was there, no doubt about it. *A .38 maybe, or, best case, a .22.*

Just as Stan readied the gun, still looking from the window, keeping his eyes on Wade Taylor, he saw him duck into Terry Kimper's house at the turn in the road. Stan scanned the stretch of land from his house to

Tuck's trailer, and Lafe Hill caught his eye, bent over his patch of lettuce, white hair bobbing in the middle of all that green like a swinging light bulb. Stan hated to put Lafe in the middle of something, but he didn't tell him to go pick late season lettuce today.

"Don't, Dipshit." Hen didn't look as puny now as before. It was her eyes, on fire and full of that gamey way she had about her when the world was still young for both of them. But everything was still good old Hen—arms crossed, hair yanked into an eyebrow-pulling ponytail, thin lips set firm.

Stan kissed her full on the lips and they didn't move against his. He lingered on her bottom lip, holding his kiss there for longer than he had in a long while. The over-under was cold in his hand, heavy and ready. He stepped out the door and Hen said nothing more. When he was off the porch and about to start across the bottom field, Stan looked back once and saw her in the window. Her arms were not crossed like before. One arm was now dangling at her side and the other was raised, a hand with fingers extended along the side of her face. He waved once and started toward Tuck's trailer.

He meant to pass by Lafe with nothing more than a nod. Lafe was good people and wouldn't think much about the shotgun, but the old man stopped him, pulling up from his stooped position and smiled.

"It's a fine batch, right? Look at that?"

A door slammed down the road, Terry Kimper's door. Wade dropped back onto the road, headed faster than before toward Tuck's trailer.

The over-under felt heavier now. Lafe was brushing his hand across the leaves of lettuce. "Let me know if you and Hen want some. I'll pick extra. Man can only eat so much. No use in wasting, right?"

Stan's eyes didn't move from Wade, and Tuck was likely back inside asleep or stoned. Lafe came up beside him. Stan saw he was watching Wade, too. "No use in wasting, but I could use some help here, Stan."

A chain link fence ran along the side of Lafe's patch, a lot where a single-wide once sat years before. He leaned the shotgun against the fence with care and took Lafe by the shoulder, squeezed it gently.

"What can I do? Where do you want me?"

Lafe smiled again and pointed to a section where the lettuce was thickest, near the middle, and Stan moved to the spot. Lafe's hands working beside him could have been his old man's, tending the crops even when he could hardly bend his fingers to button his shirt.

Stan didn't notice Brown pass them and disappear around the corner of the trailer. He always brought up his parents when talking to Lafe, and his father's old friend told a story from years ago when all the land was ripe with crops, and Stan allowed history to swallow up the present, working what was left from that time quietly.

5

It was because of a loose cannon and repentant named Charlie Sammons that Brown Bottle found himself on a Wednesday evening sitting in a metal folding chair listening to a room full of drunks and pill heads stirring around tables and mumbling and laughing, generally trying to seem normal for everyone else. Brown might not have known much about addiction theory or recovery solutions, but he knew bullshitters when he saw them.

Charlie Sammons and Wade, of course, because he had busted in on Tuck Collins. But Brown hadn't been thinking about anything other than revenge when he showed up at Tuck's. He hadn't had blood on his heart when he knocked his trailer door in and pulled him off the couch, pinned him to the wall. He had only planned to beat Tuck down pretty good, give him a reason to turn Nick away next time he showed up with money. He sure didn't plan on Hen calling the cops and them getting to the trailer as fast as they did. Turned out they had been watching Tuck from nearby for weeks. Less than ten minutes after he knocked the door in, two officers had him cuffed and in the cruiser.

So now Brown sat court-ordered in a meeting for drunks. Thinking of Charlie Sammons eased his mind, though. And, besides, maybe what little beating he managed on Tuck might just be enough to keep Nick out of all his troubles.

Charlie had donated the building in 1987. He was one year sober that year, and it had also been a good year for drain pipes. Sammons built up Sammons Drains little by little over the years, finally making a boon of cash in '77 during the worse flood in forty years. The county emptied coffers for four months buying drains from his company to fix washed out bridges. He always put in the low bid because he always knew what the other guys were offering. His grade school friend, a magistrate, fed him the information.

He took a lot of that money and bought oil properties around the region, eventually starting Sammons Drilling. He took a lot more of it and drank it, smoked it, and snorted it until crashing the next decade when police arrested him at Foster Lake naked and shivering on a houseboat he didn't own with a woman who was married to his friend, a magistrate on the fiscal court. The whole thing was a masterpiece of failure, but the drilling company thrived, even while Charlie was gone to Arizona for two months in rehab. It wasn't much different than how the place ran for the two years leading up to Charlie finally falling into legal troubles that his money and connections couldn't fix.

When he returned from Arizona, Charlie was tanned and had put on just the right amount of weight. He had become thin as bird-bone while a using addict, but now he was filled back out and had gotten a lot of sun playing golf for a month after he was released from the rehab facility. He told those willing to listen to his story of recovery, how it changed him, and he showed people, too. Before an antique car show he funded and arranged, he took a podium and gave a public apology to everyone he had hurt during his years of depravity. Anyone there would have said he was as sincere as a bible verse. Charlie became a role model, and even Brown Bottle himself thought of him from time to time while trying to get dry. If Charlie Sammons could do it, anybody could. It was likely the most common thing said at meetings all over Port County.

The only one sitting down and sitting still at the meeting was a lady in her mid-forties, Brown figured, who sat at the head of one of the long tables, the kind you see in high school cafeterias. She wore a thin flower-pattern dress that draped to the top of her ankles, sandals with toe-straps. Her toe nail polish, Brown noticed, was about the color of mint chocolate ice cream. She might have not combed or washed her hair in a month from the looks of it. Tangles sprang out from every angle, blazing out from a smooth, pale face, blue, alert eyes and thin lips. Brown thought she looked sickly and could use a couple cheeseburgers.

"Okay, let's go ahead and get started," the lady said. She introduced herself as Marie and immediately followed that by telling the entire room she was an alcoholic.

Brown leaned into the guy sitting beside him, a boy no more than eighteen. "Lordy that little lady don't beat around the bush now does she?"

The boy smiled briefly, crossed his arms and fixed his gaze on the far wall, working a pinch of tobacco around in his lip like a cow grazing, staring at the big sky.

She passed several laminated papers down the long lunchroom style table and asked that someone take one and pass the rest along to the other tables. Every one of them did exactly as they were told. The room moved like one slow wave building up and headed for the river bank. One table was all women. Brown thought they looked like the most angry and hateful women on the planet. They wore thick, dark makeup and dark clothes. They were about the only table not whisper-chatting. Men at the tables to each side of them watched the women from the corners of their eyes. The men made occasional remarks more loudly than needed about homosexuality, making it so the women could hear them more clearly, Brown figured. Mean men. Mean men and angry women all over the world.

The woman who was handed the stack of laminated pages shuffled through them in a dull way, a way that put Brown off. She might have been cleaning a rifle and homesick for the hills like he'd seen before. There was something about being homesick and holding a rifle that gave a person the same look as this woman had in her eyes. Brown figured them to be malicious and cold, and he tried to remember to steer clear of them unless he could help in some way, even if it was to get them laughing by making fun of him. Wasn't a soul in the town didn't get a kick out of riding the hell out of dirty old Brown Bottle. If he could bring this group of young women some laugher, so be it. God would remember it as an act of kindness on his part. Brown was trying to build up all of those he could, to offset the rest.

"Each table take one," she said. "And while they're doing that can I get a show of hands if you're still working step one?"

Brown raised his hand while standing up. His knees buckled back and forth.

"My name's Wade. Most you all know me. I probably should say my name's Brown. But it's not. My name's Wade. You remember me from high school, Alex. We threw that fossil out the back window of Miss Dutton's science room. You remember? My name's Wade Taylor, people. And this is a heap of bull poop."

The head lady smiled and held her hand up just slightly when a few giggles started along the back wall. She nodded for Brown to continue.

"They judged me to come here and talk about drinking and all that. Being angry and trying to kill Tuck Collins and all that. But I'd just as soon they put me in jail with Nick. That's my nephew. He's there and I'm here. They didn't judge him to go to no meetings, and he should, 'cause Tuck's got him hooked on pills and who knows what else."

When Brown stopped talking, the giggling fell off through the room. About six others, the back wall gang, were also court ordered to attend AA meetings once a day as part of various offenses. Brown never joined them in that back galley. Their plan was to float and do their time. *Just a different kind of prison.* Two or three showed up for meetings drunk, stood up and apologized and cried, promising they'd do better. Back to jail for them, and then the courts would place another two or three in the Gunther House, the halfway house for Port County, and then the Gunther administration would have those two or three signed up for meetings. Young boys, mostly. And most of them were also ordered, by the court, of course, to attend Narcotics Anonymous meetings. It was a mess and Brown was in the middle of it.

He was still standing, but didn't have much else to say, it seemed. Then he pointed to a tall man wearing a thin jacket slumped next to the three coffee pots beside the restroom.

"That's Stan Collins there, you all. Just wanted to say I got nothing against you, you understand. But that brother of yours, he's going to kill my nephew, and I won't have it."

Stan hadn't looked up from his coffee. He'd listened to Brown and wanted to stand up against him when he mentioned Tuck. He'd come to have a go at him, actually. Was going to catch him outside when all these people made a circle and did some sort of prayer or whatever to the higher power. One guy told Stan when he showed up for the meeting that his higher power was Andy Griffith. *You can have anything you want as your higher power*, he told him. *It don't have to be God.* Stan told him that was a good thing, that a man better have some options and then he moved along, found his place at the coffee pot. And now here was Brown Bottle Taylor pointing him out and speaking to him directly.

"I suppose I should've figured you'd spot me, Brown," he said. He sat up straight in the chair. "Stupid to think different now that I give some thought to it."

The necklace-wearing lady turned to get a look at Stan. "Is there a problem?"

"Yep, but we'll work it out. Step out, Brown?"

Stan scanned the room. He knew about half the people there and they knew enough about him and about Brown to understand. This lady running the show might not. He stood up and pulled his jacket tightly around the swell of his belly and walked to the door, stopping briefly without looking back to Brown, then stepping out into the evening.

The crisp scent of snow was in the air though it was the second week of October and not a flake had fallen. But it was coming. It was warm the day when Brown stepped past him while Lafe pulled lettuce up from the ground, even for autumn. Pulled a pistol on him in the back bedroom after slamming the door through. That sound, that snapping of metal and hinge, broke him away from Lafe. By the time he made it into the trailer, Brown was standing over Tuck with the pistol. Other than Tuck's scared breathing, not a sound. Hen must have made the call. Police cruisers arrived within minutes. They'd already been there once that day. Place and purpose were easily defined and to face facts, Tuck's had become a hotspot for the troopers, on the radar and a long list with other dealers in the region. But this time they had to wrestle Brown Bottle Taylor to the ground. This after luring him away from Tuck Collins, a crying and pitiful man who they wanted to arrest for dealing drugs but couldn't. Brown could have shot Tuck. He did not. Maybe it was fear. Maybe it was hesitation, which could have been the same thing, more or less. But he didn't kill him then. It was a thought. Something to go on.

Stan sniffed the air, waited for Brown. When he stepped out the door, Stan half-expected the fighting to start right away. He'd been preparing for that, but he wasn't prepared for Brown to start off with conversation.

"I got no bones to pick with you, Stan," Brown said evenly, squaring his shoulders. "But it might be that you got plenty for me, so just go on ahead and try what you think you ought to and be done with it. I settle my scores one at a time." Stan took a step forward and Brown held his hand out, spoke quietly. "Now you ought to be fair and tell me if you got a gun somewhere on you, 'cause I'll be honest and tell you I got none on me."

It all puzzled Stan more than he hoped was showing to Brown. "I ain't got a gun. But I'll tell you one thing. We have to settle this now, this thing with you and Tuck."

"That's for Tuck to settle. Not you. I said as much in there with the boozers."

"Now see, you're interrupting me, Brown. That won't do."

"Don't call me Brown."

Stan rubbed his chin and looked at the starless sky, sniffed that scent of snow, took it deep into his lungs, and tried to compose himself. "We're not getting too far with words it seems to me. Why worry about *one*?"

Brown placed his hand on the door, froze in place for a half beat, and then walked four steps across until he stood in Stan's face. "I understand you don't want me around Tuck. That's 'cause you love him and don't want harm put to him. That's how I am with Nick, and so we're just caught in some real poop here, Stan. Rock and a hard place."

Brown started back into the meeting and Stan coughed loudly. Brown turned around slowly.

"I don't think you're going to kill my brother. But, see, I can't let you do anything to him. And so, yep, we're stuck a little, but knowing you're not going to kill him is more than I had before we talked."

"Well, heck no! Good for you, Stan."

The two men stood in the chilled air. Between them a great tension welled up, like a large spring being pulled slowly apart, its thickly pressed metal losing compression and about to release.

Stan's eye twitched, a nervous ticking of muscle, and he pulled his shoulder back in reaction. Brown took this the beginnings of a move toward him and lunged at Stan. The two bone-thumped to the ground silently. They grappled in that quiet way for a full two minutes until a woman from the meeting, sneaking out for a cigarette, saw them.

The woman tossed her freshly lit cigarette and ran to Brown and Stan, poking her arms in when and where she could, trying to get some kind of grip to pull them apart. But it was no use. They held fast to each other, so she went inside to get help. It took three young men to get them apart. Only then did either make a sound. Both Brown and Stan started yelling at one another then, low-growl yelling like injured dogs. They were still growling when the lady chairing the meeting parted the crowd.

"You two. Get out!" She kicked weakly at both of them. "I'm calling the cops if you don't get out right this second!"

His arms held tightly by two of the young men, Brown relaxed and eased off. He saw Stan do the same.

"It's not my fault that nephew of his is a druggie," Stan said, out of breath. His eyes scanned the crowd.

Brown didn't answer, didn't say that he wasn't his fault Stan's brother Tuck was a drug dealer. *Nothing was anybody's fault. Everything just was, and people had to deal with it.* This kind of fighting and scuffling was part of dealing with it, messy or not. He saw Stan holding his ground and knew one of them would have to walk away first. Brown did, hoping someone would notice he was the bigger man after all. Hoping that from now on Stan would stay clear. Hoping like he always did, but knowing it made no difference at all.

6

There was a colder spark to the air when Nick stepped out from the Port County Detention Center. The mountains' bare trees reached up to the sky the color of white nothingness, flatted clouds just above the peaks like car primer boot-scraped across a dull wall. Nick couldn't see John Attic Ridge from where he stood, but he knew it was there, and that somehow made being surrounded by mountains manageable.

Somewhere in the building behind him was a file with his name on it. It wasn't as full as, say, his uncle's, but it wasn't slim reading, either. A long line of speeding offenses, a few theft charges later dismissed through a friend of a friend who knew the judge. For Nick, that process was always a far longer line of people. For him those dismissed charges started with Doug Hall, his uncle's best friend. Nick figured that to be strange enough, because Doug had a larger file than about anybody in Port County.

At some point along the way, Doug had made connections with the right people. Everybody smoked weed at some point, even if they later ended up in law school and, if they smoked, they usually went through Doug in some way or another to buy it. It was one wobbly circle of need and favors. A favor would have been a nice thing to have the last couple of days. To have had Doug on his side for this charge would have made everything easier, but this time it was more complicated than some missing sheet metal some guy forgot he even had in the first place. The county moved fast and hard on anything drug-related these days. Pills more than anything, ever since eastern Kentucky became the "prescription pain capital of the United States." Pills were bigger than cocaine, bigger than heroin. Pills were as big as it could get, and they were fifty times easier to get your hands on. If you could find a doctor to prescribe, you were in. If that doctor got gun-shy and stopped writing scripts, all a person had to do was go to a pain clinic. The doctor would usually write a referral on the spot just to get you out of his office. If the pain clinic got busted and shut down, there were always folks like Tuck. That was a wobbly circle, too, but mountain folks were nothing if not industrious.

Nick shook loose a rolled Bugler cigarette from the hard pack he had taken in with him and lit it carefully, taking a long draw. It was satisfying because it was his last. He blew the smoke skyward and again scanned the mountainscape. Time in the mountains had to be managed by everyone who lived in them, no matter status or wealth. There were few gray areas, as people say. You either saw the mountains as protecting you from something or confining you to something. Nick never understood what those somethings were supposed to be, but he felt confined more than protected most of the time. What he understood— had understood for a long time—was that there was a need for them in him and probably everybody else in Port County or anywhere else around the area. Some people needed protected and others needed to be behind bars. But it wasn't his day today to be behind bars, so the mountains looked beautiful to him, as beautiful as John Attic Ridge did when he was a little boy and could just live in them without thinking about the purpose they served. He was free either way at this very second, in a real damn way, not some sort of high theory type of free. He took one last draw from his cigarette, careful to not burn his lip, and flipped it behind him in the direction of the jail.

Getting cut loose on a one thousand dollar partially secured bond meant he would have no car when he made it back home. Putting the car up seemed a fair shake to get out of that drunk tank with ten or so other guys. He had spent two days using the bathroom in front of all of them, five feet from where he ate his dinner and seven feet from the guy who slept in the corner until just ten minutes before Nick was released. The first thing the guy said was that he had had a dream he was dying from AIDS. It had been that kind of a two-day thing.

If Nick were ever voted in as mayor of Portville or Port County Judge-Executive, the first thing he would do would be implement a county-wide taxi service, or bus service. *Hell, one van and one guy driving around nonstop would be a start.* As it were, he was walking until somebody passed by and recognized him. Recognized him and didn't really care who his family was or who he was, for that matter.

On the morning of the second day in jail, he had asked for a haircut. He had vomited in his hair when he nearly overdosed at Tuck's and hadn't been allowed a shower. He might have insisted for either a haircut or a shower a little too strongly because within a half hour a guard came and escorted him to an outer room, shoved him into a metal chair, plugged in a razor, and shaved his head as close to the skin as possible. The guard finished the whole process by taking the butt of the electric razor and giving him a good knock about two inches from the center of his crown. It swelled to a knuckle-sized knot almost the second the guard hit him. The guard gave him a wet towel, told him to rub down his head and the ugly knot and make it quick.

But all that was par for the course. Nick had come in overdosed, and if there's one fast way to get knocked down in jail it's to come in overdosed. The jailer and the sheriff both had kids in rehab for coke and meth, and they felt the public needed to see they were not going to tolerate it in anyone. The sheriff had even arrested his own son not more than six months ago when one of his deputies found him at a scrap metal yard peeling fenders off totaled vehicles and stacking them in the back of his truck. The deputy said he was so high he tried to sell the metal to him right there on the spot.

About two miles outside Portville, a truck slowed down when Nick stuck his thumb out and did the customary one fast turn on his heels. The chances of being picked up hitchhiking without turning around or without walking while you thumbed were absolutely zero. The truck wasn't familiar to him, but when he made it up to the window he saw Walk Stanton, a guy who used to be the roof bolter at a mine he night-watched after dropping out of high school.

Nick opened the door and got in. "Hey, Walk, thanks bud. I thought I's going to have to start sticking out my bare leg before anybody'd stop."

"Well, I've been in those same shoes more than once," Walk said. "Least I can do to pick somebody up in need of the same."

The cab of the truck was mostly coated in oil and grease. Empty bottles of Shell Mart brand 10W-40 knocked around Nick's feet when Walk pulled back onto U.S. 23. The old miner turned his cap sideways to watch for traffic and merged into the fast lane. When he did, Nick noticed how much the old man had aged. His Dickie work shirt buttoned to his neck forced the skin there, brown as the pan side of a biscuit, to bunch in folds, each one covered in gray stubble. And wrinkles. Nick had not seen wrinkles so deep and defined before, none like the trenches intercutting across Walk Stanton's cheeks and circling his eyes in sunbursts. Each one seemed to cut far enough to have touched bone and brought it back to the surface of his skin. His arms and legs might as well have been made of bone inside the legs of his pants, and when he breathed there was a low whine, the sort of sound a person could hear ease out from a lung black enough to get lost in coal pile.

Walk watched the road, his chestnut eyes alert despite his age. When they came to the first set of lights on the outskirts of Portville, he finally spoke again. "I hear you been running around with the law's daughter. What's her name, I don't remember. Just know she's Dan Bell's girl. Now, no offense, but how's that happen, Nick?"

Nick had been seeing Ashley Bell for close to a year now, but he wasn't sure he wanted to talk to Walk about it. *Still, Walk was probably doing nothing more than trying to make conversation*, Nick thought, *so it might be polite to say a little something.*

"Yeah, some buddies of mine said she was slumming," Nick said. He kicked one of the empty motor oil bottles with his toe. "I guess you know how that went."

"I'm guessing they ain't much your buddies no more," Walk said, a grin twitching to life at the corner of his mouth.

"You'd be guessing right, Walk," Nick said. "One of them got a little wall-eyed somehow."

Walk smiled fully. "A fair good punch landed just right will do that, I hear."

"You hear right."

Walk drove on. The conversation faded out and Nick was lost in the landscape out the window. The old coal tipple and, just past that, a stretch of land dotted with trees ending at the bank of the river. Nick was picturing what it would be like to buy that land and build a two story house with a wraparound porch with Ashley when Walk's voice carried over into his daydreaming like bark peeled from a branch.

"How's Wade been doing?"

Nick sat up in the seat and turned around fast then tried to seem more casual.

"Wade, um, yeah. He's doing okay. Getting along, you know."

Walk cocked his eyebrow at Nick.

"It's only that you're about the first person I've heard call him Wade besides me and my mom, and most of the time even Mom called him Brown."

"Brown." Walk said the name like it was a bug caught in his teeth. "Brown Bottle, right?"

"Right."

"I've known Wade since he was younger than you," Walk said. "I remember when he volunteered to head over to Vietnam, how people talked about him like he was already a hero before he'd done so much as get on the bus. A few years later, all that faded away, the television switched people's minds, the politicians switched people's minds. It was about that time Wade came home." Walk stopped talking. They were less than a mile from Garden Road. "They's some of them spit on him. People you would know if I told you their names. Same people turned him away when he went for work."

"I've heard about some of this stuff," Nick said. "But other than the spitting, most of what I've heard happened because of Uncle Wade's drinking. Can't trust a drunk, and all that."

"That's ass backwards," Walk said. "Fact of business, it's flat out bass ackwards."

The turnoff to Garden Road was a sudden dip off the main road, so when Walk flicked the steering wheel and pulled onto Front Street that connected to Garden Road his muffler grated against blacktop. Nick saw him wince and bunch his shoulders before throwing the truck into park. He nodded at Nick and Nick stepped out, nodded back and Walk pulled away. He didn't have to explain why he didn't drop him off at Tuck's trailer. A lot of people didn't want to be seen as much as sitting in his driveway. But this is where his Aspen was, as far as Nick knew, and he also had business with Stan, if Stan would listen, not to mention a word or two for Tuck for not picking him up when he came to the jail with his car title for the bond.

Nick figured Tuck was worried considering the near overdose and especially the fact he ended up in jail. There were no cars parked at Tuck's besides his Aspen, and Stan's house looked empty on the hillside. Nick went to the Aspen and pulled the door open, checked for the keys. *Nothing.* He kept walking, out through the garden corn and then up to the river bank where reception was better, and he took his prepaid cell from his pocket. He dialed Ashley but got her voicemail. The brown water pushed at the bank and the lapping of the bank waves was the only sound. He sat in a spot where he could still see Stan's house.

He fell to thinking about the two-story house with the nice big porch again. Ashley could take her photos right off that porch with one of those extended lenses, he'd build the frames with some thrown out pallets left behind the Sears and a skill saw bought and paid for. She could hang the pictures all over the house, a ton of them on the wall following the stairs to the second floor.

And every single bit of that idea was about as foolish as it could be, and Nick knew it. Ashley wasn't exactly like her mom and dad, but she was close enough. Still, he loved her. She never looked at him and saw the stories about him and his family. He checked his cell. *Nothing.* She didn't care enough right now to wonder where he was. *Best to get my mind on other things or get busy while I'm waitin' for Stan or Tuck to come home.*

The corn rows were right in front of him, and he walked slowly until he was in the middle of them. The corn was called "Gotta Have It," Tuck had told him during planting. Sweet enough to pull off the stalk and eat where you stood, he'd said. He took one off the stalk, jerking downward and toward his chest, and then shucked it clean, pulled the butt of the stalk sideways until it broke even. It was sweet and, aside from being air temperature instead of hot, he'd never had better. Even while dealing drugs and doing drugs and arguing and fighting with each other, Tuck and Stan Collins could farm. Though clearly neither did as much as they once managed when their parents were still alive.

A vehicle rumbled to the east of the bottom field. Nick couldn't see who it was for the stalks, but he could hear the vehicle had pulled into Tuck's driveway. He started a slow trot out of the field until he reached a large patch usually reserved for lettuce and cabbage and saw a Honda Civic park two feet from the front steps.

A tall man and a woman wearing a Cincinnati Bengals winter jacket stepped out of the Civic. They had added a lot of parts to the Civic—fenders, a different hood, a custom spoiler—trying to give it a racing movie look. It looked more like it had fallen through a used car lot and picked up five or six differently colored pieces as it went, a rainbow snowball of ugly and a job half done. The man had the slump-shouldered walk of many tall men around the county, as if the effort it took to move at any pace was more than their scarecrow frames could handle. The woman tilted in her shoes behind him as they both made their way to the front door. The man knocked a second time just as Nick made it to the edge of the garden.

"Nobody home," Nick called out, walking to the foot of the steps. He stopped and stuck his hands in the pockets of his jeans. The tall man turned and, even from eight feet away, Nick could see the scabs crawling up the left side of his face and the skin tight against the tendons in his neck. The woman grabbed his arm when she saw Nick.

"Where's he gone to, do you know?" the man asked.

"Never can tell," he said. "He might be gone ten minutes or ten days. You all been here before?"

The man patted the woman on her shoulder and she seemed to relax. He took the five steps in two strides and joined Nick at the foot of the stairs. When he was closer, Nick could smell the sewer gas aroma of meth coming in waves from his clothes. The man rubbed his hands together and tried a smile. Where his top row of teeth should have been were only white-raw gums.

"I'm Stephen. Stephen Eversole. This here's Candice." He stuck out his hand and Nick shook it, hiding how he rubbed his first on the side of his leg. Candice had followed Stephen down from the porch. She had smiled when Stephen said her name and took his hand in hers. "Yeah, we've come up to Tuck's a few times. You?"

Nick knew what he was being asked if he bought from Tuck. So he nodded, and Stephen continued when he saw he was safe to talk openly.

"We hit a snag on stuff for cooking, you know, cooking our stuff there at the house. It happens sometimes like that and when it does we come out and get a little medicine off of Tuck," Stephen said. Candice had returned to the front door and tried another knock. She rattled the door handle and it came open. Her face went slack and then she pulled her dark hair into a one large knot of stringy rope, tied it off, and smiled, clapping her hands. "Stephen! Stephen, we're in, baby! It's open!"

Stephen lunged up to Candice, and the two went in as if a realtor had just invited them to take a stroll through it, no hesitation, no other thought than getting into the house and finding pills and taking them.

They entered with every intent to steal. After a beat or two, Nick followed them in.

No more had Nick stepped into the living room than he had to close his eyes. Everything reminded him of the last time he was there. The two recliners placed like rabbit ears out from a large flat screen television mounted somehow to the paneled wall, the collection of various shoes and boots to the left of the doorway that clogged off half the hallway leading to the bedroom and bath. Everything his eyes touched brought a thick and stinging mess to the back of his throat.

And the smell was that much worse. The air inside the trailer was more than stale, it was a scent with weight: the oil and grease, the faint odor of pot and beer, rotted food probably coming from the dozen or so fast food bags scattered across the kitchen counter and the tiny dining room table positioned just beneath an air conditioner that had turned more dark brown than its original white and was covered in dust.

Nick had taken all this in less than a second when he walked from the porch into the living room. He opened his eyes now and the first thing he noticed was that Stephen and Candice, two addict strangers, were nowhere to be found. Nick listened for them and didn't hear anything. Then, from the guest bedroom, Candice let out a long howling sound and laughed.

"Close that door, man, and come on," Stephen said. His eyes were large and seemed about to spill out from the sockets. He stood in the doorway to the master bedroom. Behind him Candice stood back and stared into a corner somewhere in the room. She was glowing, as much as a woman in her shape could glow. She looked happy.

Nick hurried down the hall and pushed Stephen out of his way. Tuck's room was much neater than the rest of the house. The bed was tucked at the corners military style and beside the nightstand were a pair of house slippers. On the nightstand was a bottle of Bayer aspirin and an issue of *Us* magazine. There was a television on a small stand and one bookshelf that sat beside the closet door, which Candice had thrown open. Otherwise, the room was bare and recently vacuumed.

Candice was pointing to the open closet. "Show him, baby."

Stephen went to the closet and pulled a piece of paneling away from the wall. Lined along the bottom section inside the wall, positioned neatly in line with a stud board, were what looked to be five or six bricks of cocaine. Beside those were cubes of pot about the same size but double the amount, likely ten or twelve bricks tied with rubber bands and wrapped in plastic. Finally, while Candice giggled behind them, Stephen pulled a large plastic container that reminded Nick of the ones full of cheese balls he bought sometimes at the Family Dollar. This container was full of pills, all the same kind. Nick stepped to the bottle and popped the cap off, doing so carefully to avoid spilling any from overflow while he plucked one out and held it close for a better look. Oxy 10s. Every single pill in the container seemed to be oxy. It was enough for all three of them to overdose a hundred times over.

At once, Nick's felt the itch in his brain and accepted it for it was. He had just gotten out of jail and was three days—counting the ten or so hours he spent at Portville Medical Center being saved from dying—without so much as a beer. When he took in the tall man and the woman he didn't see the same things he did earlier. He saw two mouths, two noses, two sets of arms that would be taking what he already saw as *his* massive stash of drugs. *His* never-ending high and ready-made drug operation. There was no pushing the thought from his mind. There was no real urge to, if he was being honest with himself.

"I'll put these back and then we need to get out of here," Nick said. He had no intention of leaving though, only to wait until the couple left before settling in until Tuck returned. *Hell,* he thought, *Tuck won't miss a handful of Oxys. Truth be known, he'd probably give 'em to me if he was there hisself. No harm, but these people need to leave.* Nick could feel the heat coming off them, that burning core of need, an energy that pulled loose a person's ability to keep their cool, the infection of the brain's better angels that made people more animal than human.

"That's not going to happen, friend," Stephen said. "We're not leaving and neither are you, unless you want it blamed on you."

"What blamed on me?" Nick said.

"The robbery," he continued, and Candice smiled at his shoulder. "When Tuck gets here, he's going to find all of us sitting right out there in his living room waiting. We're going to tell him we came around to get some pills, found his door open, and just figured he'd ran out to the store for something and would be right back, considering he didn't lock up. Thought we'd hang around and wait on him."

He stopped, satisfied with his plan as he was hearing it aloud, and started again. "For all Tuck knows, we've only been here a few minutes whenever he shows up, even if that's two days from now. He ain't got no cameras out or nothing. We know that much. He goes straight probably and checks on this fat little stash of pills and sees they're gone. What, we say. Gone, we say. We're surprised. Must have been why the door was unlocked, we say. Tuck is never going to think we sat right here and had at his stash, took it and hid it down riverside until we could come back for it. Who would do that and then sit right here until he showed up? Nobody, that's whom. But we're going to do that very thing. So what's that add up to? It adds up to us three getting comfortable and getting high, having some of whatever Tuck's got around to eat, watching some TV. Just kicking back. And if you don't want to take part in it, then we'll pin it on you somehow. Main thing is, you ain't going out that front door and getting a chance to tell anybody about this. This is our vacation, buddy."

He turned and grabbed up Candice and spun her around. She laughed, and the two might have just been married for all the joy filling the room.

Nick sat at the kitchen table and watched Stephen and Candice flip through channels on Tuck's flat screen. They were each in a recliner and had taken a ringed plate from the kitchen and a spoon to crush pills about a half hour ago. They had snorted until both were glazed over and nothing more than a combined slur.

Nick had thought about explaining how stupid their idea was, that notion that Tuck, coming home and finding them all here, would believe the stash had been taken by someone else. He wouldn't take the time to use any sort of logic that Stephen had laid out. He would likely shoot them or some other retribution. Tuck wasn't usually one for violence unless poked at like this.

The couple's conversation went from mumbling to a much louder affair, and it happened quickly. Nick figured he must have missed the front end of whatever disagreement had led to them now arguing, but it was nearly to the screaming stage when he stood up from the kitchen table.

The two of them stopped long enough to stare him up and down and then continued talking. Quietly now, leaning in at each other from the recliners, getting their faces as close together as possible.

"I'm not putting this back," Stephen said. It caught Nick's attention. He went to the refrigerator and kept searching through the empty shelves, pretending he wasn't listening.

"We put it back and get him to come back and get it for us," Candice said. "He'll do whatever he has to do for enough money, or money we can promise him if he brings it all back to us. It's a fucking better plan than this. Only reason you want to do it this way is so you can sit there and get high now. You never think about the big picture, baby. *Never.* "

Nick closed the refrigerator door and told them he needed to step out for a cigarette, promising he wouldn't go farther than the porch. When he stepped outside, he left the front door open enough that he could hear. After a few seconds, Stephen started in with his side of things.

"He's your Mom's second cousin or whatever, babe. You don't know him. You know as much about him as any of the rest of us. He's way off the reservation. Is that what you want, handing a chance like this over to the likes of Fay Mullins? *Fay Mullins?*"

The way Stephen said the name gave Nick a jolt, and the name wasn't unfamiliar to him. His heart guttered hard enough that he felt it in his temples. He had heard of Fay Mullins. *Something from back in the day. It wasn't anything good. Rape. Murder. Something big.*

"You're not listening to me," Candice said. She slurred less and less as she went. "This sitting here and waiting for Tuck to show up ain't making a lick of sense. We put everything back, call Fay, and set this whole thing up right. There's too much in there to be half-jacking around and fucking it up." She stopped and Nick could hear her fumbling around with something. "I've got his number in my cell. Mom made me save it in my contacts before I left. In case I needed it. We need it now, Stephen."

There was a long silence. Nick worried they might have both started to wonder where he went. He gave it a three count and walked back in. Candice was gone. When Stephen saw him, he popped the recliner back and started flipping channels again.

"It's almost dark," Nick said, hoping to prod them along. He noticed Candice's cell phone was on the nightstand between the two recliners. "All Tuck has in the fridge is beer and I'm hungry. What's the score here, man?"

"Beer?" Stephen sat up, made a dramatic spin move and went to the refrigerator and took out a bottle of Bud Ice. He unscrewed and tilted it where he stood.

Nick slipped the cell into his pocket and went down the hall to the bathroom. He knocked on the door.

"Hang on!"

When Candice swung the door open, Nick moved aside and let her out. She didn't look at him, only swerved into the washing machine just outside the door. Nick watched her make it down the hall with her hand on the wall for balance and then he went into the bathroom. Inside, he took her cell and, hoping there was no passcode, turned it on. There was a picture of her and Stephen at the river smiling mostly toothless from ear to ear. No passcode. He went to her contacts and found what it was looking for faster than he thought he might. *Fay Mullins*. He flushed the toilet for show and added the number to his own cell.

"I'm calling my girlfriend, unless you all got a problem with that, too," he said once back in the kitchen.

"Go ahead, man," Stephen said. They were both at the front door putting their shoes on. Candice stuffed what looked to be a ball of aluminum foil into her Bengals jacket. "Step on out here."

Nick did as asked and Stephen pulled him through the front door to stand with Candice on the front porch. He reached his arm back inside, locked the door, and patted Nick on the shoulder.

"That's that," he said.

"That's that," Candice chimed in.

"What's that?" Nick asked. He followed them down to the patched up Civic. "What's going on?

"This is too deep," Stephen said, getting in the Civic with Candice. He looked out from the window at Nick. "We got what we need. Besides, if we want more we know where to come. You do what you want, there, partner." He started to back up and stopped, stuck his head out the window. "And best not tell anybody about this or we'll know. We got friends, and you want to steer clear of us if you can, bud." They backed up and pulled away, leaving Nick standing in the dusklight.

Nick dialed Ashley. When she picked up, he started walking away from Tuck's. "Hey, it's me. Let me run something by you, and let me finish before you say anything."

And she did.

7

On his fourth day out of jail, Nick went to talk to Stan. He was really trying to help his uncle, but wouldn't have said so if asked. He loved his Uncle Wade, but in order to avoid a fair amount of public ridicule it was necessary to create a certain amount of distance between the two of them. He wasn't proud about it, but it was what it was.

Stan sat in his usual spot on the couch. Hen was out to get a fuel pump for the car. Seemed the fuel pump was going out a lot lately. He would have handled it himself, but when it came to fuel pumps, Hen was a master. *Need to probably bite the bullet and get a new one,* Stan thought, *especially if I want to keep Hen at home for a change.* Part of him wondered if she wasn't creating reasons to get out of the house. Stan got rid of this thought, cleared his head and focused on the new hell standing outside, waiting to get in. Nick bounced up the front steps and knocked on the door. When no one answered, he knocked again.

"Stan! You here?"

Stan shifted on the couch, stuck his leg into the cushion. There wasn't a reason in the world why Nick shouldn't just move along if he stayed quiet and didn't answer. The vehicle was gone, lights were off. Give him a minute or two, he'll move along, surely.

"Stan!" Another four knocks.

"Sonofabitch!"

The couch shifted with his weight as he pulled his feet off the side. Without pulling on his boots he went to the door, opened to the screen door and saw Nick. Stan stood in his socked feet staring at Nick. The kid looked bad. He was still wearing the same shirt and maybe the same pants he'd had on when the super trooper took him out of Tuck's half gone on pills. He could make out most every bone in the boy's face, cheekbones most prominent, eyes sunk into his skull but bright. Nick wasn't high, it seemed, and he was standing on his porch.

"What the hell?"

"I'm here to talk to you is what the hell," Nick said.

"I tell you what, I've about talked enough with you boys lately."

Nick stepped toward the screen door and Stan could see he'd shaved his head since the arrest. Probably a cut he had been given in jail. He could see scabs and one two or three inch gash above his left ear on its way toward healing but still deep and pink, scabbing just starting around the edges, curling up like wilted flower petals.

"You're gonna want to hear what I've got to say. I know what you and Uncle Wade talked about. But you don't know everything."

With a sharp tug on the screen door, Stan waved his arm in an exaggerated motion toward the living room and Nick stepped through in the gloom of the house. Stan watched Nick shift about.

"Sit down, kid."

Nick did just that, easing into a wicker-upholstered chair beside the front door. "Well, I'll just get right to it. First off, I want to thank you."

"Thank me?"

"Yeah, for saving my life. I would've died in Tuck's trailer that day if you hadn't got me out of there. Second, Uncle Wade should've never been at that meeting. Just like me, he was court ordered to go to NA meetings, you know, Narcotics Anonymous. They meet above on the second floor of where you guys stood off the other night. But we all know Uncle Wade likes the drink and so he just figured the AA group was where he was supposed to be. I was upstairs in the NA meeting. They just lumped him in with the NA group because of all the drug stuff they figured he was tied up in. Didn't drug test him or nothing."

Meetings? NA or AA what does it matter? Stan thought, then asked Nick, who by this time was relaxed back in the chair. His eyes still seemed clear and his voice wasn't slurred. Stan believed he was actually straight. *A mighty feat considering I gotta pass Tuck's trailer to get here.* Tuck was out of jail without bail the next day, agreeing, he said, to be an informant in return for leniency. The thought gave rise to a question.

"How are you out?" Stan asked. "I know it's been about a few days, but still. How does that even happen?"

"Same set up as Tuck. Just took the rat way out. But I don't intend to follow through, and doubt Tuck will do any different. It's a death sentence. No different than snorting pills and what have you and dying in some pissy bed like you found me that day."

"Pissy bed" got Stan's Irish up a little. He felt his arms tensing, his hands and knuckles. But Nick was just a kid raised by a crazy mama and a cork puller for an uncle. *He came by it honest enough.* But there was still the issue with Brown wanting to kill his brother over this kid, and now here he sat in his living room, the cause for it, whether he had intended it that way or not.

"Your uncle wants to kill my brother, Nick," Stan said, his voice even and flat. "You know why, and you know what that means for me. It's like your uncle said to me a few days back, it's a rock and hard place. I can't let it happen. Won't."

It occurred to Stan just then that Nick probably drove that rattle trap car right up to the bottom field. "Where'd you park, kid?"

Nick smiled and repositioned himself in the chair. He'd been in the house about fifteen or twenty minutes. Hen would be back soon.

Whatever this was about needed to get situated soon. Hen would run this boy off so fast he'd be two counties away before the hour was up.

"I'm not an idiot, just an addict, Stan. I parked at the end of Front Street and walked up." He stopped fidgeting in the chair and leaned forward. For the first time Stan saw something other than stupid youth in his face and busted scabs and marks from getting whopped in jail. "Besides, Tuck ain't home. Just because you see that truck of his down there in the driveway, well, that don't mean a thing. Tell you what, I'll take you to Uncle Wade and Tuck right now. That's the whole point of me being here. I'll show you where they both are."

Smiling, Stan pulled on his boots without thinking of what he was doing. "Just how you reckon to do that, kid?"

" 'Cause they're in the same place right now. And I know where Uncle Wade always goes. He'll have your brother there. It's a guaranteed fact. I can't promise that one of the two of them, or both, ain't already dead. But I'll take you straight to it."

Stan had no reason at all to believe anything Nick Taylor said. *About anything at all, really. Especially not about this situation.* Despite being the reason for this whole mess, he probably understood less than anyone involved about exactly how far and how bad things could go. Still, there was a truth, or a maybe more of a confidence, in his voice. He spoke in the way of an old farmer about the weather, as if the wind couldn't blow another direction for no reason and the rain had no choice but to fall from the exact darkened cloud at the exact time it had to that day. It was an easy wisdom Stan heard in Nick's voice.

"Grab that notebook and pen beside you," Stan told Nick, and Nick handed them over.

In his scrawled handwriting, Stan left a note to Hen.

Gone to tend to business, Love—Dip.

"We'll take Tucker's vehicle, kid," Stan said. He pulled on his jacket. "And you're staying in the car." He left into a back room of the house and came back with a rifle.

"I don't think so, Stan."

"Protection, kid. Not malice. Learn the difference."

Fifteen minutes along Sandy Gap, a curving road leading into the town where Nick grew up with his mom and Brown. Not much conversation. Nick sat in the passenger seat of Tuck's new F-150 with the window rolled down smoking one cigarette after another. Bad idea driving Tuck's vehicle out to this, but it's all that was available. Nick's failed to start on three tries. *Out of gas*, Stan assumed, and they had walked back for Tuck's truck. There was an extra key under the fender.

Sandy was a once thriving small town, as much as possible in the region, before the cut-through took out traffic heading into Portville, the county seat. Part of that traffic and commerce was due to Todd McMullin, a Kentucky Mr. Basketball winner, a center for the Sandy Bobcats, and eventually a University of Kentucky recruit. Within two months, Sandy's pride and joy returned home to work at his father's auto parts store. Story was Todd got roughed up by some of his teammates in some way or another. That was in the early eighties. Within ten years they started on the cut-through of the mountain to make a new four-lane highway and the old Sandy High School gym was used for pickup games, a thrifty businessman named Edgar Turner bought it when the school finally closed to consolidation and rented it to young boys and others around town at twenty dollars an hour.

As Stan and Nick passed the old gym, Nick lit another cigarette, looked through the three inch opening at the top of the window. "I watched Todd McMullin play in that gym once," he said. All Nick could remember about the gym was that once, when it was still used for high school games, he had stood on Early Paul Thompson's shoulders and twisted his way through one of the windows on the second level. He remembered how alive the whole building felt in the dark, how secret and different from the way it felt during gym class when it was all lit up and full of sound. He had let Early Paul in the back door and the two of them played one-on-one on one of the side basketball hoops with a soccer ball they found outside the locker room. It seemed every memory he had had a foundation of some sort of criminal activity, even though, with the gym memory, they hadn't destroyed or stolen a thing. They hadn't as much as told anyone else about doing it. It was just something to do besides being bored. If he could find more things like that to do now, he would be a lot better off. The price for staving off boredom got a lot higher somewhere along the way.

Nick took a long drag and blew about half the smoke through the opening. The rest spread out into the cab of the truck.

"Roll that window down for crissakes."

Nick flicked the cigarette out the window. "It's right up here, the place where we used to live. On the right by the truck garage."

Stan knew the building, a two-story light brick building from when Sandy had been a coal camp. He had no idea what it had been used for before, but by the time Nick came into the world it had been parceled up into three apartments and a barber shop. The barber shop on the first floor was still in business. Bob Harper had paid rent there for over fifty years. When Stan pulled into the small parking area in front of the building he saw Bob come to the window. He waved and Bob offered a wave back, then pointed to a long crack in his window he had covered over on both sides with duct tape.

"We lived around the back apartment, but I don't think you can get down that little road or driveway or whatever it was," Stan said, adding, "Looks growed up with weeds pretty bad."

"That's fine. We'll just walk around and look for sleeping snakes as we go."

Before they were both out of the truck, Bob Harper was on his front step. A former Marine, Bob always wore short sleeve button-up shirts no matter the season with half the sleeve rolled twice to reveal a tattoo received while he was in service overseas. "Boys shot my damn window out with a .22, I think. Couple nights back," he said. "How you been, Stan? Hiya, Nick."

Neither had a chance to answer.

"If you're looking for Brown, he ain't back there, far as I know. I usually see him coming up this left side through the creek. He might've got past me, but I don't think so. Ain't had a cut all day. Not much to do but watch people and cars passing."

Stan rubbed his hair and walked slowly up to Bob's front stoop. "I been better, Bob. Thanks for letting us know." Nick was beside him. He nodded at Bob and looked at the ground. "How's it you figure I'd be looking for Brown?"

"I didn't. Seen Nick there with you there and thought it through is all."

"Reckon?"

"Yep, I reckon." Bob looked away from them and then back. "Anyways, you can get back there and check, but I'd take Brown's creek route there. Man might stay drunk, no offense, Nick, but he knows when to avoid a patch of weeds. Probably at least two rattler dens down that path."

Now it was Stan's turn to nod. He tipped his head and motioned Nick to the left side of the building. The left side looked worse than the right side, though there was a small, worn path down to the creek. Brown's path, Stan figured. He started down the incline and felt Nick's fingers on his elbow.

"Get your hand off my elbow. I ain't a cripple."

Nick eased off Stan's elbow. Looking back, Stan saw the teen watch him negotiate the small incline. He finished the climb beside the creek with half his boot in the water, which he quickly pulled out. "See? All fine and good. See there?"

"All fine and good," Nick repeated. "Yep." He jumped from the drop of the incline to the edge of the water running smooth down the creek, about six inches from where Stan stood, wiping mud from his boots.

The path extended more widely along the bank of the creek. Stan could see the field Nick mentioned where Brown used to play with him, show him a few old fighting moves. Nick told Stan he wasn't drinking then.

"I'd believe that when I saw it," Stan said, and stumbled on the bank of the creek. Nick took his elbow and pulled him back, then twisted it with his thumb and finger until Stan's fingers were pinned just above his shoulder blade.

"How'd I learn that, then?"

"Point taken. Now get your hands off me."

They continued into the clearing, a grown up field now with only a single worn path easing through the middle. Following the footpath, they came to a worn out section about the size of a double-wide trailer. There were empty bottles of beer and a blanket tossed to one side of the worn down area. Scattered with even less order were bags of chips and pizza boxes, curled at the corners from rain or dew so they looked more like tired and strange flowers dotting the ground. The space felt lived in, like a room or a house. The bushes and hedges were the walls, about six feet high. For the flooring, a large family of bobcats might have nested down in the space.

"He's not here, Dip."

Stan spun around as Hen parted the grown up brush with her skinny arms and joined them in the worn out patch of field. Her hair was tied loosely at the crown of her head with a handkerchief the way she did sometimes when there was work needing done. She only nodded to Nick and walked close to Stan, who backed up half a step. "What you thinking about, Dip?"

"What are you thinking about?" Stan shot back. "What the heck are *you* doing here?"

"Oh, for crissake, I'm trying to keep you from doing something stupid. What else? This boy's uncle ain't got nothing against you. It's Tuck he's got a problem with. Since when did Tuck's problems start being your problems? Our problems?" She looked quickly to Nick. "And exactly what in the hell are you doing here anyways?"

Stan let what she said sit for a bit, roll around in his head. She was only trying to do right by him, but some things were complicated to put into words, even to someone you love. Hen cocked her head to the side, waiting for some kind of answer, waiting for something.

"Nick here told me Brown would have Tuck out here, fixing to kill him," he finally said. "Told me it was a fact. I can't stand around if somebody comes and tells me something like that, Hen. I've got my gun, but just for protection. My only intention is to see that my brother ain't killed. What's so wrong with that?"

A breeze building from the ridge tossed Hen's hair down from the crown of her head so that thatches of it slapped across her forehead. Stan could see the deep grooves and wrinkles there and knew he was responsible for most of them. She squinted her eyes together and gazed across the field, silent. Without saying anything more, Stan moved to her and took her elbow. "Okay. Let's go. Let's go."

They moved away from Nick and crossed back over the path and were out of sight without turning to see if he followed. When they were out of view, Nick walked to the far edge of the field, took four steps left of a budding redbud and stomped the ground firmly with his boot. There was a puff of dust and then the ground opened, a grass-covered square tilting into the sunlight. Suddenly Brown crawled out and stretched long and hard.

"They gone?" Brown asked.

"Would I roust you if they was still around?"

Brown kept bending his knees. His hair was more of a mess than usual. He scratched at the crown of his head long and hard and started off across the space of field. His shoulders were slumped more than usual, boney and tired under the skin, the mechanic's shirt he always wore. Each step seemed a task of its own for his legs, two crooked limbs broken in half at the knees.

"What were you going to do to Stan if Hen hadn't showed up?" Nick asked. He'd been tasked with getting Stan there to the field. "All this fighting, it's my fault and I wish I could do something so's it would just go away."

Nick watched Brown's step quicken. He almost wondered if his uncle knew himself what he was trying to do and exactly how he was trying to go about doing it.

"This is just strange as strange gets," Brown said. "Just as strange as can be." He seemed to drift away while they walked toward the steps of the apartment. "It is your fault, bubby, but that don't matter. And I'd rather not fight Stan, either. Thing is, I got to get my point across to him. But all that's not the strangeness I'm talking about."

Nick ran to catch up. "What are you talking about?"

"Listen, son, I'm privy to the fact that Hen's the one been taking your money and giving you that mess of drugs about every week or so," Brown said. He didn't turn around to face Nick, and Nick didn't stop walking, but they kept to themselves the rest of the evening. It was so much to take in that Nick felt the need for a fix come on him stronger than ever. It was a bother to him that Uncle Wade knew about Hen being his dealer. *Who else knew, and how long would it be before Stan figured it out?*

When Brown was into his cups for the evening and just about to nod off, he answered Nick's unspoken question in a slur. He said, "Stan might just try to kill us both. We got to figure something out." This was followed by short bursts of snoring and soon after, the drawn out sleep of the drunk.

It wouldn't have mattered if Nick had an answer by morning. When he woke, Brown was gone. Nick knew he would need to find him soon, but, truth be told, he could use a little time to himself just now. He could use a nice, smooth high.

8

A spot behind the library, shaded by a small tree and overlooking the back of the Big Sandy River—Brown knew this was where Blair had her lunch on warm days. So, in October he didn't expect to see her sitting on the bank watching the brown water of the river run past. But there she was. He wondered if she would figure out some way to keep having lunch there when everything turned to winter. He hated to imagine her wasting her life in a break room in the library eating a sandwich and missing the coming of spring. It put a hole in his heart to think of her that way.

Brown saw her as he crossed the bridge, moving in the direction of the library. In his back pocket was the envelope with Mary's address written on it. He didn't need the phone number now, of course, but it gave him an excuse to see Blair. That she was outside having lunch gave him pause, and Brown stopped where he was on the bridge. He stood still and watched her until she saw him, waved him over.

"Hi," Blair said with a smile once Brown was close enough to hear.

Brown waved his hand, tried to appear calm. He was sure she could tell he was nervous. He stood with his arms at his sides a few feet from where she sat on the grass and focused on the rivers current, swift and determined on its way to the sea.

"Did you get hold of your sister?"

"Sure did. Yep."

"Good, that's good."

The silence hurt like a sunburn. Finally, Blair patted the ground beside her.

"Sit right on down, if you want." She smiled again.

Brown did as she asked. When he sat beside her, Blair tossed her hair over her shoulder. He fought the urge to inhale deeply the scent of shampoo and flowers, honey, something fruity and light and wonderful. She wore a blue spring dress with a cardigan sweater. There were small goose bumps on the back of her calves, still tanned from summer.

They sat for a full thirty seconds without talking, both watching the river. When she took a small bite of a Slim Jim, Brown cleared his throat.

"I'm going to give her another call today," he said. "I use this lady's phone who lives just down the road here a piece." He pointed over his shoulder, noticed the only thing his breath smelled like was strawberry icing. *Left over from Janice's. No alcohol*, and he was especially glad considering he was sitting so close to Blair.

"You can just use the phone in the library if you want," she said. "They have this long-distance coverage where you can call anywhere in the country and it's just one flat fee for the month. I'm not sure really what it is, but I know the bill's the same every month, and sometimes I have to call places like Colorado."

Brown nodded and Blair stood up. He rose and fought off the urge to tell her he loved her. Stopped it on its way up from his lungs and cut it off inside his throat. But he wanted to, more than anything. Instead, he motioned for her to walk ahead of him and was content watching the curls of her hair dance from left to right between her shoulder blades as they walked the parking lot back to library.

It was strange to be in the room behind the counter, the place Brown had first seen Blair sorting books on the table in the middle room as he passed through to check out the movies. He dialed Rusty's number. It rang once and someone picked up.

"Hello, Wade."

"Mary? How in the world did you know it was me?"

"It's this thing, caller I.D. It shows the number a person's calling from and I figured wasn't but one person would be calling from a library in Sandy."

And just like that, Brown lost the urge to plead with Mary again. It was her voice. Not only was it distant, but, worse, uncaring. Maybe it had always been and Brown was only now noticing, but something about her voice was final. Brown decided to speak to her as if it would be the last time.

"I'm going to these AA meetings," he said. "Trying to quit the drinking, for real this time. Figure if I'm going to watch after Nick, I can't do it drunk. But I'm not going to bend your ear about all that. Just wanted you to know."

There were a few seconds of quiet on the other end. Brown waited it out.

"Well, that's good, Wade," Mary said. "Maybe if you're sober at least some of the time that'll be all the help you all will need."

Brown stifled himself from saying anything mean. He thought of Mary when she was young. At one time, Mary smiled more than anyone in the family. Before their father left, he used to get all of them to sit together in the living room and have Mary do what he called sketches for them. It mostly involved Mary dancing and singing random bits of songs while dressed up in their mother's clothes. She was good, or she at least made things good for a while.

"Nick's going to be okay, Mary," he said. "Still, if you ever want to get hold of us, maybe call this number. Blair will let me know you called."

"Who's Blair?"

He almost told her. He almost tried at least telling Mary he loved Blair, but she wouldn't understand and wouldn't care. He wouldn't waste something like that on her. There wasn't another second he intended to waste on Mary. He hung the phone up.

When Blair popped her head into the doorway from the front counter, Brown could see she was concerned. The softness in her eyes nearly gave him courage enough to tell her, but he just smiled and thanked her for letting him call, then asked if they had *The Breakfast Club* on VHS.

9

Low light made it difficult to tell if it was dusk or the slow breaking of morning. The silence Nick realized was the absence of bird chatter which usually hinted to early morning in the woods of Yellow Flats. The flat area was once used as a road for hauling coal from the mountain in hatefully loud short-bed trucks, but now it just made for a fine place to let go and be scrubbed clean of worry and all the terror of the world below. It seemed a Neverland without a leader, without conflict. Certainly without innocence. There were Indian burial grounds all over the place, folks said. Nick had never found as much as a flint of broken arrow. But not long after they cut some trees along the top line of the ridge for lumber last summer, the couple weekends after that did seem different somehow. More restless. *If the ghosts of Indians roamed Yellow Flats last night, they're probably still high on a contact buzz,* Nick thought.

He had gotten wiped out fast in order to drive away the gang of nameless burnouts pushing their half-hearted warnings off on him. They knew about the cops, the days in jail, and the detoxing he'd come out with. Most of them knew the cops took him out of Tuck's, too. *More warnings, more advice.* Without exception, every one of the seven or eight who partied with him and Ashley the night before had also made the comparison to his uncle. "Brown, think of Brown," they said. "What happens if you wind up like him?" And each time, they stopped afterwards and looked to the ground or off somewhere else. It was easy for them to forget how he took people talking about his uncle. They probably didn't remember until they saw the look at his face after saying it. On an even day, some of them could kick his ass, likely, but not when his anger was stored up over his uncle. All of them, too, had seen him crack Pearson Newsome's head open with a stapler in junior high for making those kinds of remarks. They all just forgot sometimes, and let something slip. Nick allowed one or two remarks like that, but only if he had been drinking or high. Everybody there was lucky he was both last night.

So a ringed dinner plate to save the pill-crush from sliding off the side, two joints and half a fifth later, those warnings were only murmurs standing over a fresh grave. Each movement from the chilled ground might have been Nick's fingers repositioning the loose dirt walls of that grave, whipping aside slabs of rain-thickened mud. But it was no use. This grave, this moment among the thick woods of Yellow Flats, this cold spot near the black scar left on the ground from the bonfire the night before, sucked around his boots and held him in place like a common sandstone.

Ashley was still asleep. When he was able to stand without wobbling, he eased down to the far end of the clearing where she had flopped on a blanket, a spent lightning bolt having lost its bright cut across the sky hours before. She smiled in her sleep, moved one foot across the other. The dark morning air smelled of vodka, sour mash and, faintly, old wood gone soft with years of rain soaking through the bark and into the ageless soil and rocks beneath the roots. She had urged him to make up a place to sleep at the north end of Yellow Flats and away from her after he started grabbing at her, touching her hair, whispering sweet and not so sweet things along the lobe of her perfumed ear.

With his head aching, Nick moved away from the patch made from the bonfire, through a small collection of young trees and to the cliff no more than fifty feet or so out from the clearing. Once he stood atop the cliff, the ache and what he could now see was, in fact, early morning and Ashley's meanness stripped away from him. A low fog covered everything below, leaving but three or four mountain tops visible. The valley cradling the areas of Flatwoods and Big Fork was an ocean now and the mountain tops strangely colored icebergs. As the topridge breeze kicked up, the fog moved like the slow motion waves of the sea. Nick looked out to the farthest tip of mountain in the distance and imagined it was an island, imagined living there and never speaking, never getting to know a single soul. He took it in, distracted only when he felt the palm of a hand brush against his lower back, a playful finger hooking for half a second into his belt.

"Pretty ain't it?" Ashley said. Her hair was perfect in every place save for an area at the back of her head that had rat-nested through the night back and forth deep into whatever she had used for a pillow. There was no sleep lag in her features. She might have just arrived, lips full and bright and without lipstick, eyes alert and in constant motion across the oceanscape of fog.

Nick dug at the corners of his eyes with dirty knuckles to push loose the matter built up there. "Yup. Never seen it look like this from the Rocks. Uncle Wade's down there somewhere. Either there or across the hill into Teller County. Likely across Town Mountain to the Teller and Port County line. But I don't know have a clue really."

It was the most Nick had said to Ashley about Brown. Their relationship had been, like so many others early on, physical and with little discussion, other than where they could get dope when the vodka and mash became too boring for the adventurous and tolerant. Their first stop when they decided to move up from pot was Tuck Collins, and now there was the stash he found with those pillheads. And not only that, but his plan having to do with that stash. And not only that, but the fact that he had shared that plan with Ashley. It meant they were moving things along, sharing important information and making promises to see things through together. Thinking of Tuck and his uncle, of Ashley and how she seemed different but in a good way to him now, Nick eased out to a safe place on the thinned flat rocks at the edge of the cliff. He sat down.

"Everything's a mess for me, babe," he said while still looking across the draped white of the valley, the bowl shape formed millions of years ago. "We have fun, but there's some things happening you can't be part of. I mean, we're together on the big stash and all that, but it's the stuff with Uncle Wade and the Collins. Tuck Collins mostly. That is dangerous of a whole other level, and you shouldn't be within a hundred miles of any of that stuff."

Ashley didn't say anything. She took a spot beside him, her legs positioning with the grace of a dancer warming up in some mirrored room far from the top of any mountain. For a spell they didn't speak, just watched the fog lift skyward the way kids in Port County sometimes watched coal trains passing, a transfixed exercise in allowing your mind to focus on one thing that leaves room for not a lot of other thinking or worrying. Just the slow and steady movement of things on the earth.

Ashley at last broke silence. "There has to be something to make things better, right? When'd you last see him, your uncle?"

"There are some things that can be done. Likely'll have to be done," he answered and pulled his knees together. "More days since I seen Uncle Wade than I care to think on."

She was the only daughter of the Bells, a family still wealthy thanks to a sharp and hardworking grandfather who started with a hardware store before buying up most of the land surrounding it. Half the people in Port County bought or leased property from Cab Bell. Even the grade school where he and Ashley once went to classes sat on property at one time owned by her grandfather and then sold to the county school board for a price not made public. Her father, Dan Bell, had owned the IGA grocery store and that kept him and the rest of theirs well fed most of the time. He stopped doing that from boredom a few years back and they took him on at the sheriff's department as a deputy. But she didn't know about these kinds of troubles. Making things better in his world often involved actions Ashley had only seen on television or maybe read in books. After the grocery store, her dad didn't talk much about what happened outside their front door, and that was plenty in this town.

"Folks know about your uncle and Stan. I know about what happened to you at Tuck's," she said. She scanned the fog lifting. Houses were nearly visible now, floating peaks of shingle and dented tin. "I know more than you think I know. I know more than that bunch at least." She pointed back to where half dozen of their friends still lay, blue noses and drunks fallen across the old auger road where coal was once hauled off the mountain, that flatness a perfect false ridge now.

"Ocean's drying up," Nick said, pointing into the valley where the fog burned. "It'll be gone soon." He wanted to ask how she knew anything about him, other than birthmarks and scars, maybe how long he brushed his teeth in the morning or what he ordered when they went for lunch on Wednesdays. There never had been secrets in this town. Foolish to think it could be any other way. He focused on the valley below. "Damn, what a nice white ocean."

Ashley gave him a confused look, the mess of hair at the crown of her head tossing gently back and forth from the wind circling the Rocks. Her bottom lip was a hostage between her teeth. "Ocean?"

"Nevermind," he said. "Just my crazy coming out."

Ashley was good to look at, and he liked her. She didn't seem to mind his dish-water hair and the fact he only washed it when his head started itching. She didn't mind his eyes, set just a touch too far apart, or his long and clumsy arms, always knocking things over or accidentally serving an elbow to her ribs during sex. But she knew about things he never told her, and that wasn't something he could overlook.

"How you know about any of that?"

Ashley didn't hesitate. "From Mom," she said. He might have just asked her what time it was.

Nick took his clumsy arm and wrapped it around her shoulder, used the palm of his hand and fingers to flatten the bed hair at her crown, smoothing it out as gently as plucking flower petals. *She loves me. She loves me not.* He had hidden things his entire life, but this was going to be the first time it came up with Ashley, keeping away his dealings with Hen, not Tuck. That Tuck's was just a place to crash like any of two dozen other places around the county and not the only place he depended on for getting dope. Whatever he and Ashley had was no longer just physical and fun and light. It was secrets that sealed people to each other. It didn't matter in the long run, no matter how sad it all was. Stan was out to get his uncle, and that was the more pressing issue.

"We're going to see your mom," he said. "And then I have to find my uncle before anybody else does. Maybe she knows something I don't."

"Anybody else? Stan's after him, far as I've heard. Tuck's the one should be worried. This guy, Fay. He seems like the real deal."

He kissed her before she had a chance to invite herself along once they had talked to her mom. Whatever notion Ashley might have to help him find his uncle would rise up and be gone like the fog by midday.

The Aspen tossed out exhaust fumes from start to finish, fogging over the two-lane through Donovan's Creek. The title went up for his surety get-out-of-jail bond, but the friendly judge allowed him monthly payments so he could have his car back to "get on the right path." Nick made the curves fine enough, focusing on the road and keeping the corner of his eyes in check from wondering to Ashley in the passenger seat. He could feel her looking at him. Normally he would welcome it, but just now it picked at him.

She rolled the window down a couple inches and lit a cigarette.

"Wanna take a couple regular?"

Ashley took two Oxys from a wad of tin foil that had been tucked into those tiny second pockets inside the real pockets on jeans.

Without a notion to stop anything other than keeping his uncle from getting gut shot, he put his hand out. "Regular will do on the road, I reckon," he said.

He put the pill on his tongue and then rooted it around until it was lodged between his inner cheek and the gum line, the same way chewers did with tobacco. He secretly preferred taking Oxy regular instead of snorting. But instead of just shot-glassing them straight away like others did when they took them regular, he preferred pouching it away like this. The outer coating melted away and the medicine would ease out and the swallowing would start and then every bad thing stopped for a while. He wasted more chances to drive away the bad things by sneezing out perfectly fine Oxy trying to take care of a line off this coffee table or that kitchen counter than he cared to remember.

Nick continued driving the two-lane, counting seconds, collecting minutes in his haze. Soon the two-lane along the creek turned to a one-lane and then from blacktop to gravel and from gravel to dirt. The dirt road signaled to Nick that it was time to slow down and look for Ashley's house.

Her folks lived fine in a nice house at the end of the creek. It was a good setup, off to itself and tucked into the mountain, not a neighbor for better than half a mile. How Ashley ever made it off the creek and into his world Nick could not figure out. He wouldn't have rebelled against a mother who was a nurse making plenty of money and a father who stood with integrity as a deputy sheriff known to get along with folks from every walk of life, pushers and preachers alike. It took that sort of makeup to deal with people if you found yourself working law enforcement in eastern Kentucky. Everything became political, especially police work, as officers often needed inside help from the same flock they intended to split apart and jail when everything was said and done.

"Dad's not home," Ashley said. She arranged her things in her lap. A purse, where she stuffed the tin foil, toothpaste and a tampon. After a second or two, she pulled the toothpaste back out and squirted some between her teeth. She swished it around then handed it to Nick. While Nick took some for himself, she tossed her hair back and forth and checked it in the mirror.

"Mom's no doubt here, though," she continued. "Probably in there on the phone already this morning making the gossip rounds. Guess it paid off this time, though, all her tongue waggling."

Ashley, talking with that sound to her voice like she was excited about their plan, gave Nick a deep wounded feeling in his gut. Sharing things with her was always going to be difficult. His life was not something he could share, never was. He knew that as far back as he could remember. His uncle made that clear and his mother was even more adamant. On the one hand, he had his uncle explaining they were different, his family, and that people were going to talk about them but to pay them no mind. Likewise, his mother had her far darker version that always fashioned the bitterness into a thing of workable hatred.

"We'll see what she knows," Nick said. "After that, well, I'll figure it out."

Ashley's eyes fell to her lap. She didn't look again to Nick before opening the door, only waved to him to follow.

The house spread out over the property like a battleship made of brick and trimmed in rich woods. But, unlike a battleship, this place invited you in, said come to the front door and nevermind taking your shoes off. You're at home here.

The place couldn't have been stranger to Nick.

A novelty wooden cutout of a police officer was set up beside a pair of wicker chairs. A set of chairs with thick cushions and a glass top table between them sat in the middle of the porch. Potted plants taller than Nick bookended the entire set up, which, to Nick's eye, seemed lonely. He wondered how often the three of them sat outside and had a snack or whatever families did on their porches. *Probably never.* The same could be said about the yard. Neatly trimmed and lined with those solar-powered lights that illuminated the surroundings just enough to see where to walk. If Dan Bell cut his own grass, and he probably didn't, that was probably the only time anyone stepped foot in that yard. The entire place had the look and feel of a banker's home, not a cop's.

Folks were always so proud to be cops, yet Nick knew that about eighty percent of the cops in this county were outlaws in their younger days. It takes one to catch one, and all that. Nick wondered what kind of hell Ashley's father once raised.

Ashley walked straight from the front steps and opened the door. Nick had forgotten for a moment he wasn't trespassing, that he was a guest and that Ashley lived in this sprawling thing of a house. She disappeared into the dim insides and left the door open. Giving the welcome mat a couple swipes he followed her inside.

Her mom found Nick before he found Ashley. She was a tall woman and seemed youthful, bouncing through the hall from the kitchen, her hair in ponytails. *Some sort of midlife crisis situation*, Nick figured.

She gave him a long hard look and then smiled as fake as he'd ever seen anyone smile. "I know you, Mr. Taylor," she said. "I'm Lana." She stuck out her hand and Nick shook it lightly the way his uncle had always instructed. *Firm and fast for a man and soft and easy for a woman and you should have no troubles.*

"Ashley's mom," he said. "Hiya. She came on in and I was just following trying to figure where she went to."

"Probably went straight to her bedroom. You should be good to go on in since her dad's not home," she said and then gave him a wink. "And don't worry about leaving the door open."

Creepy enough, no doubt about that at all. Nick watched her tilt off through the hallway back to some room where she would return to sitting in a chair, he imagined, legs crossed and eyes half-lidded. He'd seen the look before.

Ashley eased around the corner. "You coming?"

"Hey, does your mom drink or anything?"

"What? God no. She's just sleepy all the time."

Sleepy, yeah. Leave it alone, he thought. "Well let's have a talk with her about some of this and I'll be going. How about it?"

A dog barked from the yard, three times and went quiet. Ashley's eyes disappeared again, looking now at the floor or beyond it. If he didn't know a little better, he'd think she was prone to pouting. Nick felt more and more out of place standing in Ashley's big house with her sleepy mom and him spilling out his box of rocks for everybody to pick over after a long time of stashing them away.

They moved into the kitchen. The image wasn't as Nick had pictured it. Lana Bell was at a chop block counter, one of those island deals with stainless steel sink, refrigerator and the all the other works circling it like petals. Lana held her head up by cupping her hand beneath her chin. She smiled when they stepped to the counter. Nick felt Ashley's moist hand wrap around his and he allowed it. Neither spoke.

"Well, here's the lovebirds," she said. "Want something to eat? We got things to eat."

She's high. Nick was too nervous earlier to make it out clearly, but he'd seen enough of it to spot, and usually faster than with this otherwise perfect wife and mom. *The whole thing is going to be useless.*

"I'm trying to find my uncle, Wade Taylor," Nick said. Any hope he might have walked in with was gone, and he didn't care if it showed in his tone.

"Brown Bottle?" Lana looked past them now. Her eyes became more focused for a moment.

"I'd just soon you not call him that, if it's all the same," Nick said. "I mean I know you're going to other times, but maybe just not when I'm around."

Nick set his jaw just enough to maintain a respectful way about himself with a touch enough to show Lana he was young and yes most times wild, but serious.

"Good enough, I guess." She stood and walked from the counter into the adjacent living room, picking out peppermint candy from a glass bowl on the coffee table. She patted the cushions beside her.

Ashley let loose his hand and waved him to follow. They sat on the couch, Ashley beside her mom and Nick at the other end. The couch was soft enough to give him a deep craving for a nap, and maybe whatever Lana Bell had stashed away. Nick was thankful when Ashley made it straight to the point.

"Nick's trying to find his uncle and I thought maybe Dad had mentioned something." She paused. "You know, something you could say that wouldn't interfere or whatever. We thought it'd be best to ask you, Mom, cause of Dad being the law and all."

"Dad being the law and all," Lana repeated, her voice dropping to a whisper that hissed peppermint across the room. She didn't stand up, but straightened her back. Her eyes became more focused. She leaned forward to look directly at Nick. "You got some nerve, you little heathen."

Her voice changed. Nick had pegged her as one of those mountain people who visited family in Ohio or Indiana and came back saying *creek* different, saying *crick* instead. Pronouncing everything slowly and deliberately, like the people on the evening news. Now Lana's southern drawl was full and thick, and the words streamed out like spring water.

"Did I stutter, you drug mutt?" she spit at him. "Get out!"

Ashley had yet to say a word, but she was holding Nick's hand back. It was damp and the grip was hard. *That's it.* He stood up, trying hard to keep from calling her a hypocrite, and stepped around her crossed leg, one foot bouncing up and down casually, relaxed, not budging to make way for him.

Walking back through the kitchen with all its stainless steel and then the hallway with its framed black and white photographs, Nick was less in awe of his surroundings. *It all seems like one huge mask now, and an ugly one for that matter. Ashley must be sneaking around to see me*, was all he could figure. *Why would she bring me here, then?*

On the porch, he gave the wood cutout of the cop a little flick on the nose, grinned and set his mind back to finding his uncle. The metal snap of the door opening turned him from his car door. Ashley stood on the porch. Even from a distance he could see tears standing in her eyes.

He opened the car door and sat down roughly in the driver's seat. Before he pulled into reverse, regret settled in his mind, fit and solid. He knew if he looked to the porch he would see Ashley crying. But the blood pushing through his veins would only allow for driving. Driving as fast and hard as he could, like a good heathen.

10

Brown twitched his toes and saw the whiskey ripple. He snorted and scrubbed at his lips. Might as well be watching for catfish bubbles. Tad Newsome told him he could get drunk soaking his feet in whiskey once. They were sitting outside the gas station and Tad was bored, Brown figured, so he concocted this big tale about dipping your feet and getting a good buzz going instead of drinking. Tad didn't laugh when he said it, he just looked straight ahead with his crow feet eyes. Brown had kept from laughing then, though he wanted to badly.

It wasn't funny at all now, with one week dry and four AA meetings that turned out to be nothing more than skinny boys trying to impress skinny girls with how bad they'd all been, oh so bad. It wasn't right to judge these kids. Not Christian by a long stretch, but at this moment, humped up in the gone to heck cabin he built twenty-some years ago on the back side of John Attic Ridge with his feet wrinkling up in perfectly fine whiskey, he couldn't focus on young folk trying to get dates.

Stan Collins was out there, and Tuck Collins was still giving Nick the drugs. The whole thing was tangled up something fierce. All he was trying to do was send a message that'd stop what was happening to Nick, the big mess he'd run straight into headlong. He didn't plan on shooting Tuck the day they hauled him off, just scare him. *If I wanted Tuck dead, Tuck'd be dead.* He hadn't even taken a shot, just held the old boy in place on the couch with that peashooter. When Tuck had picked up the phone and dialed for the cops, Brown let him, although grazing him across the shoulder had occurred to him, if he were to be discussing that day between just himself and the Maker. But there was less meanness to him than people understood. By a long shot, that was the case. Life had put a darkness in him, an anger. What it took just to survive. As for bothering others, Brown was happy to leave people alone, let them have their vices and problems. The lady at one of the meetings had said it best. Some little guy was jumping onto another guy trying to tell about how he had lost his girlfriend and so forth, and she told that boy that it wasn't his circus, wasn't his monkeys. *Not my circus, not my monkeys.* That's how Brown usually left things. But when it came to Nick, he didn't feel that option. He had responsibilities.

A big fine mess, Brown thought, and pushed the washtub away from him. He took a hard look at the shifting whiskey, the way it glinted brown in the half-light, and stepped from the cabin, his throat burning from memory and longing. Outside the cabin, he stretched and turned to his left. The ridge curled out in line with the smooth vanishing of the mountain, crested with poplars and the occasional small grove of pines. Squirrels jumped from tree to tree and stopped with each jump. Brown couldn't help but smile as two squirrels raced one another from a limb and crashed to the ground in a snap of brittle leaves. He squatted low and just as he had always done, lay his hand out hoping one of them would cross by accident, imagining the scared creature resting for a moment in his palm.

Thinking of the squirrels and hearing the other wildlife around him, the flutter of brush across the mountainside and from a distant point in the neighboring valley a woodpecker hammering into the dried belly of a hollow tree, Brown rose to his feet, wanting badly to curse and wondering who was around to be offended if he did. Well, he knew. *I'm here and God's everywhere.* His sister had said it so many times before Ohio.

It would be two years this winter since Mary moved with Jim Chapman to Ohio. This was how it was supposed to be for her before she ended up at their uncle's house all alone. Shepherd came in talking Bible and Mary just went right away for him. Brown tried a few times to warn her off, but Mary only saw scripture and Jim Chapman's easy brown eyes. That's what she called them, easy brown. *Dirty brown, more like it.* He knew Jim Chapman, and Jim Chapman was no man of scripture. He used to give it a good go on Wednesdays and Sundays as a deacon at Beth's Creek Freewill Baptist Church. Brown went with Mary on more than one occasion and saw firsthand how Chapman got up behind the lectern and led the opening prayer. He would sing too loudly with the choir and then walk back and forth at the pulpit talking about how this one or that one didn't listen to Jesus, how they never really got Jesus' message. "It's all about love," Chapman used to say. And the whole time he would be eye-balling women in the congregation. "Love," he would say, drawing it out like he was aching from his loins so bad he couldn't stand it another second.

And all those women, including poor beloved Mary, went for the whole act. One big damn lie right there in the house of God, right under his nose. It was told Chapman bedded some of the women in the church. In a room behind where they baptized people, the room where most people changed out of their wet clothes after receiving the gift of salvation, Chapman was said to have hammered it out with at least three women, women of the congregation. All of them married at the time. Brown confronted Chapman once, about two weeks before he and Mary left out for Ohio. Chapman left understanding in no uncertain terms that if Mary was ever hurt in any way whatsoever, there would be several shades of hell to pay.

Chapman had acted cocksure about it in front of Mary, but Brown saw his body language when she wasn't looking. His body said he wouldn't do a thing, at least not anything he'd let Brown find out about. It wasn't the assurance Brown wanted, but it had to do for then. Finding out Mary was at Rusty's when the first letter arrived meant more business to settle once all this with Tuck Collins was situated. Debts of the heart were always stacked past a man's ability to ever catch up.

"Dammit!" His voice rolled away from him in layers of echo. And though his heart was some lighter for it, his thoughts turned back to Chapman and Mary and Ohio and, most of all, to Nick.

Mary had come to him then with the news on a Wednesday. He was on his back in the field breathing vodka fumes in his sleep. She said she was moving with Jim to Ohio where he had a job waiting. Brown remembered how her face was blurred and the sky behind her a gray smudge from his wavering vision. Mostly sleep, but a lot of drink, and he couldn't make a road sign from a moose. "Ohio," he had said. "Ohio," she answered. There was no mention of Nick not going, and so he felt the loss on that level. It wasn't until Friday that he found out Nick was not gone.

For nearly two full days Nick went wandering around Sandy like a dog dropped off on Abner Mountain and left to die. It never made sense to Brown why he didn't come home to the apartment, unless he figured everybody had lost their minds and gone. The gas station crew is how he found out Nick was still around. Nick came in there early Friday morning saying he stayed all night at Timmy Jameson's house but nobody had cooked anything. He was hungry and asked for a snack cake. When Brown came in later that afternoon, they told him about the whole thing. They looked at him with even more contempt than usual when they did. When he went back to the apartment, he found Nick in his bedroom sleeping. They never talked about those couple of days, and when he asked about his mom, Brown told him she was doing what she thought was best. A lie about that didn't matter much. Nick knew better.

Now, surrounded by trees on the slant of the mountain, Brown thought of Nick and how he might have been better off in Ohio with that rotted Chapman. They would have eventually ended up at Uncle Rusty's anyways. But Brown knew when they hadn't heard from Mary in three months or so, things had gone south. He thought then she would have phoned or just come home, but she never did. When he phoned her in Ohio was the first time he'd even tried to get in touch with her. Brown once imagined her living a nice, Christian life, attending some dried up church where they probably didn't even play guitar and piano, cutting the grass on land so flat it would make a man's stomach turn. Nick insisted Ohio wasn't all that flat, but Brown just told him he was missing the point. But never too harshly, never anything too harshly.

"It's my fault," Brown told the trees.

He was moving along the ridgeline now, following the auger road. The cabin was behind him, the waving whiskey light, and he was alone in the hills. He snapped a branch underfoot and listened for the squirrels to fetch away, expectant of hunters, no matter the season, probably most afraid of the Branham boys from Glich Creek come over the valley into Port County. If they couldn't find something to shoot, they'd roll down onto the horseshoe main stretch that ran through Port County and see what was loose they could steal and take to Handy Creek Trade Center and sell.

He came to a peak jutting out from the hillside large enough to have a good rest. He looked down at the horseshoe shape of his town, sat, and pulled his knees up to his chest. These peaks and the ridges dotted around them were the strongest parts of the mountains, holding off from being beat away by weather and time because what they were stronger than the sediment rock. *They must be made of iron to stand up against all that power*, Brown figured. Sitting on his favorite now, seeing the town below just a tiny curve with the barber shop, the truck garage, and the old high school the size of his fingernail, he felt so small.

When he couldn't take feeling that way anymore, he climbed off the peak and found a water gap cutting a path of least resistance to make a baby valley inside this larger one, and he dipped his hands into the steady flow. He brought up two handfuls and gulped. *Nothing. Tasteless.* His body might appreciate it, but it was doing very little for the thirst in his soul. The cabin was a short walk back. *I still got legs, and the goshdang washtub is still flopped on the floor waiting.*

He found a Styrofoam cup someone tossed out while four-wheeling or heading up to Yellow Flats for a bonfire stuck on a tree branch and tucked it under his arm, careful not to pop a hole in it while he made his way back. Soon the drooping cabin was in view. The sun hadn't hit the cabin full on yet, and the washtub would still be cool.

Brown pulled the door open and it jarred loose at the top right corner. He nodded and then shook his head. No concern either way. He gave the washtub a little nudge with his boot and the whiskey sloshed around. His knees popped loudly when he bent to dip the cup in, and, still bent over, sniffed the brim, felt his throat tighten with anticipation, the back of his throat watering up already. A long drink and another and the cup was empty. The whiskey burned in that wonderful way, and his stomach was warm in seconds. He dropped it like a penny into the tub, watched it spin for a bit and then come to port along the inner edge.

At some point, on some strange day, he or another of the crowd he ran with then put up a mirror in the cabin. Probably it was Cash. He deejayed for 104.3 The Rock back in the seventies and was mostly concerned with his hair looking just right, long and divided into two ropes over his shoulders the way Willie Nelson looked without the braids. Cash was in a band and said he needed the mirror in case he ever had to leave the cabin for a gig. His band never had a gig that Brown could remember.

But there hung that mirror still. Splotches like mold or something had collected from the corners toward the middle, but Brown was able to see enough of himself in it to feel a fair amount of disgust. No more than the usual amount. He scratched at his chin growth. *Did a rat eat your razors?* That's what his daddy would say. He wished his chin jutted out more like Clint Eastwood or James Dean or whotheheckever. Instead, you could barely see his chin, it hid so far back against his neck.

He stretched out his neck so his nose nearly touched the mirror.

Mean eyes, though. Strong, don't-mess-with-me eyes. The sort of color to them able to catch fire any second. The only thing that'd saved him more than once standing off with all sorts of no-counts was staring a guy down. When it didn't work, he had to hurt them. Sometimes they got him pretty decent.

He turned his head. *Half a lobe missing on the right ear. A rough night, that one.* Guy from Williamson took offense to something Brown said and charged him. Didn't take a swing or throw up a knee or nothing. Just went straight for his ear with the few teeth he had left. And then this Williamson boy took off running. Brown stayed behind until the cops showed, looking around the place for that part of lobe like it would matter if he found it.

He smiled into the mirror. *Rough night, that night.* The Styrofoam cup was floating in the tub of whiskey, setting sail again. Brown pushed it down and let it fill up then pulled to his chest, switching it to his left hand so he could wipe dry his other on his pants. Two gulps in, he heard the cabin door give way a slow splinter-creak.

"Hey, Brown," Tuck called.

Tuck looked even smaller in the doorway with the big trees behind him. He'd lost twenty pounds at least in the last year, about the same length of time since he'd had a haircut. Brown saw a good full growth of beard, thickest at the no-count's jawline.

"Rat eat your razors?" Brown asked, and sat back in one of the cabin's three chairs. He finished off the cup of whiskey. "I'll offer you a drink after we take care of this. Should be a straw or two somewhere around here. You might be able to get a sip or two through."

He almost felt bad for Tuck Collins right then. *Small and frail, even if it is from his own doin'. Nothing but a snack for a good fight with him that puny and in that condition.*

Tuck didn't step into the cabin. He took a step back and held out his arms in the way a man will when he's trying to show he means no

harm. Flannel drooped off his wrists and elbows, the bend at his armpit.
A bored scarecrow stuck in the middle of the woods. But his face was
all harm, as much of it as you could want.

"I've got boys up here with me," he said. "Outnumbered mean
anything to you, you drunk?"

Brown was up fast and closing the distance between the two of
them.

"They'll shoot you, Brown. If I lower my arms to my sides, soon
as they see you they'll shoot you. And then you know what? We'll take
you up to Spider Town and haul you back in an abandoned mine."

His mother, Heaven accept her, didn't raise no fool. Brown allowed his
retreat to be a slow turn back to the washtub to dip the cup again. He
landed roughly back into the chair, hating that he wobbled and showed
he was feeling a buzz.

"Go on ahead and say or do whatever you figured on saying or
doing when you hiked your lazy butt up here then," Brown said. "If you,
in fact, got boys out there with some old creaky rifles or shaky little
handguns and so high from your pills and whatever else they couldn't hit
a bull in the butt with a bass fiddle, then let me ask you something, Tuck."

Tuck stood with arms still out, Christ-like, satisfied with himself,
the power of the moment.

"You think that's something new to me?" Brown continued. "Try
laying snake-belly on flat land and knowing they's well-kept machine
guns twenty feet from you and men holding them so focused you'd
think the Lord himself was putting a bead on you for them."

For less than a second, Tuck's easy grin went flat, and then returned.

There hadn't been a single bird take flight, not one of his squirrels
from earlier move off in another direction. There had not been a sound
from outside the cabin except Tuck's yapping. Brown figured he was
bluffing, but it wasn't worth it.

"This whole thing has to do with Nick," Brown said. He could
feel the whiskey in his words. He kept back anything else he might say.
He would allow Tuck to either kill him, which was unlikely, or talk himself
down and leave.

Tuck stood in the doorway a few beats more and then stepped
inside the cabin. Not a muscle on Brown's body moved. He was ready,
either way. But it would have to be Tuck who would take him down. He
knew that wasn't going to happen. And so did Tuck.

"You ain't scared of dying?" Tuck said.

Brown sat in his chair. He shuffled his feet, doing a little dance on
the rotted boards, smiling.

"Talking too much," Brown said. "Got a gun on you? Pull it out,
aim it at me, and shoot. Do that, or get out. Do it now, or get out."

Tuck lowered his arms. Brown could almost see embarrassment across his face, like the underbelly of a fish, white and vulnerable. When Tuck turned to leave, Brown pulled a .360 from his ankle holster and winged Tuck in the shoulder.

"On second thought," Brown said, and then listened to the wildlife scatter through the hills.

11

"Raise your shirt, Mr. Mullins."

"How about I just take it off?"

"That'll be fine."

The nurse asked him to breathe heavily three or four times, moving a stethoscope from his chest to his back and then to his chest again. She moved the stethoscope slowly under his shirt. Fay flexed as the cold circle moved over his skin. He hoped her finger would brush him. There wasn't a lot of opportunity for romance for him these days. He had to make moves when and where he could. Time was a commodity in his business. And secrecy a much larger one. One-night stands were more common when he was a younger man. The whole process was easier without wrinkles and bit of overhang at his belt buckle. Fay didn't much mind, though. It came with the life. When he was younger, there was still nothing that could be lasting. A life alone was the price to pay, a price worth the sacrifice.

And the nurse was fine looking. Green eyes, bouncy blonde hair with highlights running through it like dripped away bits of honey. He could smell her perfume a full minute after she walked out. It had been months since he'd enjoyed the company of a woman. Staying away from home could be difficult in several ways, but that was one of the worst.

When she came back, Fay slowly took off his shirt so she could see the scars and how nicely kept together he was for a man of his years. It was the tattoos she mentioned.

"That's a phoenix, right?" She pointed a red lacquered fingernail at his chest. Fay could feel its sharp tip shaking a few of his chest hairs.

"Yep."

"Interesting."

"Why's that?"

"It just is, I guess," she said, stepping back and bending her head to write quickly on a chart that she cradled against her waist like a flatted out child.

"It just is," he mimicked, and then smiled like a fly trap. The assistant looked up and turned her head sideways, the way cats will from time to time. "Maybe it's interesting because that's the mythological bird of rebirth," he said then. "Born again and again from its own ashes."

The assistant's small lips dropped open and Fay could see her teeth were white and straight. He continued to smile warmly at her and leaned back against the wall, the stiff paper stretched across the exam room table crinkling as he did so.

He hadn't counted his scars, but there were more of them than tattoos. There was the biggest scar and the one he was most proud of just above the phoenix, a thick and shiny one that curved across his chest like the body of a lizard. A half dozen or so more were scattered out across his back like a series of islands. Many more on his hands and forearms. These were the brightest of them all against the leather brown of his skin. Fay had obtained not a single one of his scars during fights, not bar fights, at least. The assistant finally commented on the one above the phoenix while taking his blood pressure.

"Looks like that might have hurt," she said, and squeezed the pump on the blood pressure machine.

Fay figured the doctor would be in soon and his little conversation would come to an end, so he talked fast and, when he did, his accent came out more pronounced than usual.

"That one nearly took out my beating heart," he said evenly, rubbing the muscles that seemed to crisscross across the bones of his arm like bark. "It was January of 1969. I was nineteen and walking with my da in the civil rights movement."

"On Washington?" the assistant asked.

"No, love. The one from Belfast to Derry." He paused and smiled again. "Belfast, Ireland, honey."

"I thought you talked from somewhere else," she said, her head turned like a cat again.

"Still a little I guess after all these years here in United States of God's America," Fay said. "That's where I was born and raised, in Belfast, Northern Ireland. Been here nearly four decades and I'm pleased as hell that it still sneaks through here and there."

"Oh," said the assistant, the inflection of her single syllable somehow more knowledgeable now, but she kept her head tilted, the honey-dipped hair curled across her shoulder, the folded wing of a sleeping bird, golden feathered even in the fluorescent lights washing down the walls of the exam room.

"We were part of what they called the People's Democracy, though that didn't mean much to me or anybody else my age," Fay continued. "My older brother used to tend bar and then one day he was shot dead as a nail by some folks on the other side. That was in 1966, the start of the Troubles. All I knew was that vengeance was heavy in my heart, but Da was a peaceful sort. So by January of 1969, like I was saying, me and Da was marching from Belfast to Derry as a civil rights movement effort or some such thing when were attacked by what they called loyalists in Burntollet, County Londenderry. Nearly every scar you see on my body happened in less than half an hour."

Standing up from the exam table, Fay held out his arms and turned in a slow circle. When he had made a full turn, the door opened and a man in rimless glasses and a neatly trimmed beard entered the room, a quizzical look melting across his eyes and down to his mouth. The man tugged his white coat closer around him like a military general about to give orders to a field full of ready troops. Dignified. Wanting it to be known that he was clearly in command. The assistant stepped aside, but continued to look at Fay's upper body, who had left his hands out to his sides and smiled out of the corner of his mouth to the doctor.

"Mr. Mullins?"

"Yep."

"You can have a seat there on the table and put your shirt back on," said the doctor. "I'm Dr. Randall. What seems to be the trouble?"

Fay glanced to the assistant and smiled knowingly, gave a soft, gravely laugh.

"Well, Doc, I work the railroad line from Kentucky to West Virginia, have for twenty years or more, and they seem to think I might've spent up my time," Fay said. His accent was gone now, replaced again with the more familiar east Kentucky twang. "They wanted me in here for a checkup."

"Seems like you have put some hard time in from the looks of it, but you seem to be in pretty good health otherwise," the doctor said. "Of course a full screen could include an MRI and some other tests, if the company has asked for a complete exam. But it says here," the doctor paused and flipped pages on his chart, which he did not cradle like a child but held it out in front of him like a shield. "It says here you can't have an MRI."

Fay winked at the assistant. "Why's that?" he asked.

The doctor balanced the chart in the palm of his hand and used the other to hold steady his glasses, bent closer to the chart. "Says here you have obstructions that would put your at risk due to the magnets in the machine. An MRI machine works in such a way that..."

"I know about how they work, Doc, all due respect," Fay said cutting him off and fastening the last button on his shirt.

"Have you had operations before?" The doctor pressed on. "Metal devices implanted during a surgery of some kind that's not in your chart for whatever reason?"

"No, Doc. Nothing like that."

The doctor turned to the assistant and gave her a disgusted look. He tucked his chart under his arm. Wordless glances were exchanged momentarily and then the doctor excused himself after handing a note to the assistant. He hadn't worked the railroad in years, actually. He didn't like this doctor, but he needed the sign off. *The railroad's a one deal, but there's new work to be done. New and old*, he thought. *This work coming up's older than the railroad work by far and far and far.* Folks around Port County, they thought they knew things about him, about his work. They only knew a little, and still it was his biggest weapon, that fear, the panic. Fay honed that fear daily, hourly. The rest of it, the weapons needed for what he did, came with the scars.

Without hesitation, Fay could still name the five techniques, the five methods the British security forces used for interrogations: subjection to noise, deprivation of food and water, hooding, deprivation of sleep, and wall-standing. For the most part, boys took prisoner were only ever subjected to one or two of these at a time, but all five at once was not unheard of, even in court proceedings. He could still remember the fourteen Irishmen taken and given all five techniques and the torture trail later. Courts ruled it didn't amount to torture, the hell-bound pricks. Those fourteen, they went through the five for a full week.

"That young man could use a drink," Fay said after the door closed. "What's his little note say?"

"You're so full of it," the assistant said, tossing her hair back.

Fay closed his eyes and took in the perfume, sliding across the air to him in a small and powerful wave. He figured to himself, *Dr. Whatshisname's good and pissed about not having all the information, his full arsenal there for his guidebook.*

"You're so full of it," the assistant said again.

"I just need a clean bill so I can go back to work. This is only my second trip to the hospital. The first time was for a physical when I got hired on at the railroad. Wasn't much to that, just cup and cough, eye test, that sort of thing. What's his little note say, honey? I got to keep this job a least a few more years. Retirement and all, you know."

"His little note says get an x-ray, STAT," she said. It came out in a hiss, the honey-dipped feathers turning to snakeskin before Fay's eyes.

"What'd you mean, saying I'm full of it?"

The assistant put the chart back in its motherly position on the soft curve of her hip, gathering herself, and left the room.

Fay stretched out a little at a time on the table and waited. For some time he whistled a tune into the silence of the room. Beside the sink at the foot of the table were some magazines and when his back muscles started knotting he pulled himself up and started thumbing through one, glancing at pictures and listening for voices outside the door. Presently, the assistant came back with another expressionless woman.

"Let's get you down for an x-ray, Mr. Mullins," she said softly, routinely, her voice as flat as an ironing board.

Fay turned to the assistant and gave her another warm smile then leaned in close, taking in her scent, feeling her green eyes on his neck as he whispered in her ear.

"That's what they'll find, honey," Fay said when he was upright again. The expressionless woman was holding his elbow, a slight tug. "And then it's just more troubles for me."

"You're just so full of it," the assistant said. It was an echo by now, bouncing off the walls of the exam room. *Void of any meaning. Just something to say.*

"Ashes to ashes and back again," Fay said as the flat-faced lady guided him through the door and away down the hallway.

In the parking lot, Fay lit a cigarette and took long draws until a security guard came by and told him smoking was not permitted on hospital grounds. *The little punk*, Fay thought. *The little punk in his plastic boots.* He smiled at the guard and held his cigarette out in front of his eyes, watching the smoke curl up and away. When he was sure the guard was watching too, he stuck the cigarette into the side of the guard's neck. The guard bent double and, when he did, Fay hit him once behind the ear and the yelling stopped.

He was ready for work.

When Fay got home, only the living room was still warm. The fall chill had spread across the rest of the three-room house after the stove fire had laid down into embers while he was gone for his checkup at the hospital. He went to the coal pile down the hill from the back porch and brought up a full bucket, fist-sized pieces and one larger to add once he got things going. He put gloves on inside and popped the door on the stove, tossing in seven or eight pieces and then watching the slow heart of the dying fire ease them into a finger-sized flame that gradually built around the little mound of black. Once building it properly, he settled into his chair by the front bay windows. They looked out on nothing but the hillside across the way, the tool shack he had raised before leaving the last time to stay low for a while. Only this and the mud road that passed in front of the house. The road extended on into the hills before dead ending in one direction. The other direction led the four miles downhill to Route 460 and on to civilization.

Civilization was what he had been trying to leave when he bought the head land of Wildcat Hollow. He brought with him from Ireland all of his savings, made up in large part from selling various guns and ammunition he had collected during the Troubles. It was enough to buy the land and build the house. Enough for a new start in America in a place he'd always heard reminded people of the old country with its rolling hills and pastures. And the people were descendants mostly of his country, clannish and hot-tempered, independent.

Since the time he settled there, Fay had grown to dislike most of the people in the area, but still loved the land, the ancient mountains, especially. He figured his dislike of the people came about naturally, considering most of the dealings with anyone usually came about through some terrible reason—adultery, theft, revenge, and, more so recently, drugs and greed. With this climate afforded for meeting people, the chances of disliking them became more likely. An easy thing to do, over time.

The doctor and nurse had stirred some old memories loose in him, and Fay regretted going at all, but it was needed. Checkups like that were a once and awhile thing for him, usually before taking a job. He'd been in Kentucky about two years when he had a heart attack, nearly dying. They went in and put a stent in his right coronary artery. Since then, he had paid more attention to his health. *One couldn't earn a living in poor health, certainly not in this business.*

After catching his breath and taking in the soothing notion that he was finally home, he pulled his boots off and sat in his stocking feet. The fire had built nicely and the living room's even warmth was easing steadily throughout the house. He went to the kitchen and made a pot of coffee, standing by the kitchen table until the pot was finished, then taking his cup back with him to his chair. As he settled, he tried to remember the last time he went for a checkup. It would have been the last job he worked. That would have been more than five years ago. It recalled his first hired job. Somewhere he had written down everything that happened during that first job in one of those composition books. He groaned his way up from the chair and went to the bedroom and searched the one bookshelf. He found the book and turned to the beginning. He hadn't dated the entry, but there it was, his four paragraphs about Sam and Arlene and all that insanity and horror and what ended up being a pretty low payday, everything considered.

Sam and Arleen lived in a section of Port County called Half-Moon Hollow, or just Half-Moon. The area was more or less a one-lane dirt road leading from Route 460 about a half mile to a coal tipple. Past the tipple was a section of land no bigger than the space filled by a Super Walmart. On the section of land were about six or so houses. It had once been what people would have called a smaller version of a coal camp town, with the miners employed at the tipple and their families living there for close access. Sam and Arleen's house was a yellow, single-wide trailer positioned along the very middle of the easternmost hillside that made up the bowled confines of the hollow's ending point.

Neither worked, but that wasn't uncommon in Half-Moon. The tipple had shut down decades earlier and the people living in the remaining homes were mostly unemployed. During the day, Sam and Arleen would spend a lot of time fighting and arguing, mostly over money. Sam had a disability from a mining accident that had taken about half of his left hand. He received a monthly check along with a Medicare card and was working on a scheme of some kind to get black lung disability, even though he had only put about a year and a half in underground. There were lawyers who could do that, he told anyone who would listen.

Arleen was listening. Also without work, she relied on Sam's checks each month, but hated him in a mortally unholy way. Everyone not only in Half-Moon but also in Port County knew he beat her beyond recognition on a semi-regular basis, usually when both happened to be drunk or high at the same time. At one point, Arleen had had enough of the beatings just to be able to get Sam's disability money and looked to have him killed, but in such a way the checks wouldn't stop coming, at least for as long as possible.

At the time, Fay worked odd jobs fixing houses, roofing or interior work in the winter, usually with a small crew of about three or four people and somebody in charge who had negotiated whatever job they had at the time. He had been in Kentucky about three years from Belfast and the crew leader, Arleen's uncle Danny, knew a little of what he'd been through, some of the things he'd done by a few conversations here and there. Danny pulled him to the side on a church shingling job and told him to drive up to Arleen's that evening after work, that she had something to talk to him about.

Fay added the large chunk of coal to the stove and closed the door. He went to the front porch and called his two hounds. When they ran around the side of the house, he poured from the bag of dog food and they started nudging each other aside, eating as fast as they food hit the hardwood. He stepped back inside and rubbed his hands together, thought of Arleen and how shapely she was then, even as a middle aged woman. Dark hair, green eyes, and a nice, wide smile full of healthy teeth. She was slender and wore cut off jean shorts and breezy shirts full of spring colors, and sandals that showed off her painted toenails.

When he made it her trailer that evening, Arleen asked him in then turned and walked with a twist to her couch and plopped down, crossing her tanned legs one over the other and started directly in on what she needed done. He was mesmerized listening to her lay it all out to him in a calm voice like she might have been having any regular summer talk with any regular guy off the street. But when she finished and Fay asked about money, she knew then he wasn't just anybody having a talk. She told him the job would pay ten thousand dollars, money she would have as soon as the bank made good on her putting the trailer up for the loan. She could pay a thousand up front as sort of a retainer. Even then, he was smart about promises. Ireland had taught him more than fighting. He had her sign a statement saying she had hired him to kill her husband and sign it. She didn't want to, especially after he explained if she didn't come through with the money his next step would be to get the statement into the hands of somebody who would care about this sort of thing in a state or federal sort of way. But she did, she wanted rid of Sam that badly.

A week and two days later, he was outside the little yellow trailer again in the dark of night, quiet in a patch of raspberries, watching for rattlesnakes and waiting for Sam to come in from town. It was the first of the month and Arleen said Sam would be liquored up by the time he got home. He was, and it was an easy thing to do it and get him into the back of his own truck and to the mouth of the old mines less than a quarter mile away at the tipple.

It was near time for supper. In the kitchen Fay found a can of Vienna sausage and half a sleeve of crackers on top of the deep freeze. There was deer meat in the deep freeze, but a laziness has set in on him and he didn't feel up to starting or finishing any cooking. He washed a fork under the faucet with a sliver of hand soap, rubbing the tines with his finger and thumb until they squeaked, and ate the sausages standing in the kitchen. Eating the last one, he thought of Sam's fingers and how they had looked after he had snapped them clean off with his own bolt cutters.

That was the second part of the instructions from Arleen, taking his hands and his feet for prints in case somehow the body was found. The first part was make sure he was killed clean in the trailer before loading him in the truck. None of it was particularly easy, but the killing, by comparison, was not so bad. For the sake of saving time, he took the fingers and toes instead of the hands and feet, and finished with the head. Arleen made it perfectly clear she wanted his head taken. She said dental records would be hard to find if nobody could do so much as locate the head they were stuck in. He used a cap wedge of a twenty pound sledge hammer for that, making sure to keep down on noise at the late hour, even hidden into the hill at the mouth of the mine.

But worse than the murdering and all the cutting and chopping was Arleen's final order to find whatever means necessary to get the body no less than two breaks into the mine. It was the hardest thing he had done up to that point and was still the hardest thing, physically, he had pulled off since. It was full daylight by the time he emerged from the mine having dragged Sam's body with nothing more than a left behind scoop cushion and a length of rope more or less from his hands and knees, considering the mine started at low coal, maybe chest high at the opening.

Arleen asked for Sam's fingers and toes, but said she didn't want anything to do with his head, to get rid of it and make sure it was gone for good. He was sure when he was finished that no one would find as much as a hint that Sam Pennington had ever exited on the planet. Like everything else about him that was cruel and sharp when it came to evil things in this world, Fay brought getting rid of bodies and body parts with him from the island.

Part of his reputation, part of what had given him consistent work for the past decade and a half, was the promise that the job would be done. There were a lot of botched kills throughout the eastern part of Kentucky when the work fell outside his control. Six or seven years ago, a man from Perry County was shot point blank in the head and left for dead in the middle of downtown. Problem was, the bullet had traveled between the man's scalp and his skull halfway across his head and exited the same way it had entered on the other side. The whole thing left him with only fingernail-sized contusions on both sides of his head. He identified the guy who shot him and saw him arrested and convicted of attempted murder.

Now, it's true that a situation like that was a rare one, but part of doing a job right was minimizing the chance for something to go wrong. If you choke a man until his heart stops beating and then cut him up for disposal, that's not something he's going to get up and walk away from. Doing the job right wasn't something he did as much as a point of pride and to increase business as he did with survival in mind. Screw up a kill and that's the end of any chance for a life free. It's most likely prison walls from that point on. And Fay had no interest in adding prison time to his resume.

Finishing the last two crackers in the sleeve, Fay got up from his chair and tossed the empty sleeve into the coal burning stove to watch it curl and blacken away into nothing. His stomach rolled over. Could be he was hungry enough for some venison after all, and being hungry was always sure to kick lazy's ass. One of the dogs yelped from the porch. The two of them were forever fighting over something and biting at one another.

The two of them were snapping at each other over one of the logs split for firewood. Fay eased over to where they were pitted against each other, trying not to cause alarm and send them running off before he could raise his foot and bring it down hard on the head of the one nearest to him. It's face bounced off the wood of the porch. It gave a weak whimper and then lay still. The other one had seen what happened before tucking its tail and heading around the back of the house in a mad dash. Fay, satisfied they'd learned their lesson, went back inside.

The deep freezer was filled with mostly bagged green beans and ears of sweet corn. Of course beneath that, in the same place he'd kept it since buying the freezer at Sears years ago, was Sam Pennington's severed head.

"Hey, you old cuss," Fay said. He pulled the bagged head from its place at the bottom and inspected it. Same look on his face, that tiger look of a man trying to get the best of another one and failing. It gave Fay a warm feeling to see that expression from time to time, a reminder of just what he was capable of at any given moment.

After a time, he tucked the head back into the corner at the bottom of the freezer and brought out two venison steaks and an ear of corn. He was hungrier than ever now and the evening had fallen into the quiet place made just for men feeling around for nothing more than a meal and a little rest.

He cooked and finished his meal before an hour had passed, then took his time walking through the house, rubbing his belly under his shirt. All that fussing with himself and general laziness about getting off his ass and making something to eat always seemed a pitiful thing to look back on when his stomach was full and his general person mostly satisfied. He felt better having eaten, always did. He sat in his chair and turned on the television. Local news came and went, and night worked slowly across the head of Wildcat Hollow. When he had to turn the lamp on beside the chair to read his mail, the sense of fullness became a tired string of moments where he mostly scanned over the envelopes without much thought. He was going to bed earlier and earlier lately. More signs in addition to his health that age were beginning to work on him, that he wouldn't be able to keep working at this rate. This always depressed him, forcing him to thinking about one big job he could ride out on.

Once he felt the food was well settled, he went to the tiny room at the corner of the house and rolled onto the bed, the only piece of furniture in the room. Just before he nodded off, he reached into his back pocket and took out a slip of paper. He felt above his head until his fingertip grazed a raised nail head and gouged the paper onto to where it rocked for a couple of seconds and then came to rest like a tiny frameless painting askew on the otherwise bare wall. He had written the boy's name down on the slip shortly after talking with him earlier in the day. He knew him, knew the boy's family. *Nick Taylor.* He said the name a second time and closed his eyes in the dark.

12

Dan Bell could have pulled into Stan's driveway from the main road, but instead turned his cruiser onto Garden Road and circled around to the gravel parking lot by Stan and Tuck's large garden. Hen knew he could see the heads of pot plants reaching skyward above the corn rows. Tuck started prepping his guerilla grow area in the bottom field way before planting season. It was always in the exact middle of the corn, because corn grew the highest of any other crop they had, he had said, as if knowing this was something akin to understanding dark matter in the far universe.

But damn if Tuck couldn't grow weed, Hen thought, looking at the tips of the largest plants showing just above the corn. Back when he still tried to get Stan to go in with him and plant patches, before he switched to prescription for pain killers and all the rest, Hen recalled how Tuck would guerilla grow in the actual way it was usually done, hiking to an out of the way place in the woods. Going barefoot the last three-hundred or so feet to the patch to keep from making a worn path. Avoiding big roots from nearby trees when planting the seedlings so they didn't have to compete with them.

She knew most of this from Stan's very nearly going in with Tuck on selling weed. But it wasn't his nature. Guilt wouldn't let him do it, even though he wasn't sure where the guilt came from. She supposed he always felt the three of them should have been able to keep profitable the garden his father left them, something they could earn a living from over time. *It wasn't meant to be*, considering Stan was more inclined to metal and tools and Tuck, though as talented a farmer as their father, was too happy to be high as much as possible.

Another day and we'll be talking about those plants, Hen thought. The fact that it always fell to her and Stan to deal with Tuck's dealings had been a sore spot for her. When they first married, Tuck was already buying and selling, on a smaller level, and she addressed this with Stan then. They camped up on Yellow Flats for their honeymoon, and Hen remembered staring at the stars and trying to bring up the subject of Tuck in a gentle, loving way even then. Stan would hear none of it. He understood who his brother was, and how hard it was to deal with him, but his brother was his brother, his family, and if she didn't want to be in the family, he'd heard annulments weren't hard to acquire. That was out of the question. She calmed him down with a long bit of loving and that was the last time they really talked about Tuck in that way. It was something to be accepted, like the movement of the stars. Beyond her control.

She watched from the kitchen window as Dan removed his hat and tossed it onto the passenger seat of his cruiser.

It was a fair walk now to get to Stan's house, but that would normally give them time to see him coming. Sometimes folks needed that, and Dan needed them to know he was here to actually help. Hen knew the routine.

She didn't try to roust Stan from the bed. He'd been drinking since before daylight and was sleeping it off. She just slipped in and slapped her hand across the foot of the bed.

"Stay in here, Dip."

He grunted.

"Stay in here and don't get up. Law's here. It's Dan Bell. I'll handle it."

When Dan knocked on the door, Hen stood on the other side for a short while before opening up. Dan's eyes were hollow, his hair wasn't combed like usual. She couldn't see that from across the field, but Dan Bell wasn't looking too good. She didn't speak.

"Stan around?"

"He's resting. What can we do for you? What can we do to assist you this morning?" Hen laid it on thick, that bite she had honed over the years.

"Can I come in?"

"Must be serious if the porch won't do."

Dan stood still, hands at his sides. The wrinkles around his eyes were like broken veins without color, sheet-white like the rest of his face. Hen stepped aside and he lowered his head and walked into the living room. Hen tossed a newspaper from the couch to the recliner, and Dan sat down. He rubbed his hands across his thighs. Hen could hear the polyester scrubbing against his palms.

"Just get to it, if you don't mind," said Hen. Despite herself, the way Dan was acting was confusing her, causing her to feel sorry for him somehow.

"Yeah, yeah. Nick came by my house the other day while I was gone for a meeting down to Frankfort. He showed up with my girl, Ashley."

"Okay. And?"

"Well, I know how all this is tied up, Hen. Stan and Brown have got it out for each other and it's 'cause of Nick coming down this way for drugs. I don't know why Stan's got to throw himself right smack in the middle of it, but he has. It's his brother's problem. Tuck's the one Brown's after." He stopped when Hen crossed her arms and looked away, through the window at nothing at all. "This boring you?"

"No, no. Not a bit. It's just you ain't saying nothing I don't know, speaking on *ifs*, so to speak. *If* Tuck was doing anything like that, I mean.

People know there's trouble with Tuck and Brown. They ain't never liked each other, really. And Nick? Hell, Nick ain't been right since the fourth grade. What are you here to tell me? That's what I'm saying. Tell me something I don't know."

"Well, here's something you don't know," Dan stopped and gazed long at Hen. "Stan's fixing to get into it deeper still." He paused, but Hen continued looking away from him, so he continued. "Fay Mullins might come into the mix somehow."

Stan shadow-walked into the living room. His shirt sagged loose from his body revealing a swelled and white belly. He made a small attempt to flatten his tangled hair. "Fay Mullins?"

Hen and Dan didn't speak. Stan hadn't looked so worn out since he and Hen spent two months in South Carolina fixing peeled back roofs from Hurricane Katrina winds. It was the only year they had let the garden go to nature, but it paid well. When they got back, Tuck was growing pot and already seeing two different doctors for pain pills.

By the end of that month, Tuck had more traffic in his driveway than the Riverview Movie Complex, a quarter of the garden taken up with weed, and was moving into other counties to add doctors for his pill supply.

"Stan," Dan said, and stood up. "I'm just here as a courtesy. Off the books, so to speak."

"Off the books," Stan said. He rubbed the stubble flaring along the sides of his face. "Courtesy. Sounds strange and a might like bad business to me. Why don't you folks at Post 9 just go ahead and arrest Tuck." Stan dropped into his chair. When he did, his pant legs rode up. His shins were hairless and buckshot riddled with specks of scabs. He scratched them absently. "That would fix everything, more or less, and then you wouldn't have to be here in my house saying the name Fay Mullins and scaring Hen."

Hen pulled her shoulders back. "I'm not scared of Fay Mullins, Dip. There's but one thing I'm afraid of and that's damnation. I just wouldn't want to have to take the train with Fay Mullins to get there. That'd be the only thing worse."

Dan adjusted his polyester pants and repositioned himself on the couch so he was leaning closer to Stan. "I see what you're saying, but it ain't that simple. It's not just us looking at Tuck. The feds are involved, too. With this Flamingo Pipeline running up from Florida, things have been made complicated. The government wants more than a search warrant and a couple days questioning, which is about all we'd get if I arrested Tuck right now, this second." He paused, then turned to Hen. "Pardon me, but Fay Mullins recently visited one of the doctors who's been providing Tucker with pills for several years. We think it was sort of an information gathering sort of thing."

As was his custom, when talk turned so explicitly to his brother's enterprising, Stan went quiet. Secrets were rarely so black and white in Port County. They were mostly gray, but there was a cutoff point for speaking of them openly.

Still and evenly, Hen said, "You think Fay's out to kill Tuck like on another one of those contracts he ran off from a decade or so ago?" She kept straight, shoulders square. "And I ain't scared of the man, like I said before."

Dan nodded. Fay Mullins had arrived in Port County about fifteen years ago, this talkative man who spent most of his time at Jensen's Real Country Club drinking and talking up divorcees. There were a few spats at Jensen's, and Dan had been called to one about a month after Mullins showed up. Ellis Edwards was dead as a hammer in the parking lot when he arrived. A crowd of drunks and rubbernecks were circled around Ellis's body, so Dan couldn't see until he split the crowd that the old C&O employee had been cut across the throat. The cut was jagged, but from ear to ear. In the very middle of Ellis's throat was a pinch of neck bone peeking through. It had been a hard cut. A little more pressure and they might have been gathering two parts of Ellis for the coroner's office.

When he wrote the report later, Dan hesitated to include this new guy, Fay Mullins, who was one of few who weren't gathered around Ellis gawking. He had been leaning in the doorway to Jensen's, a bottle of liquor in one hand a milk glass in the other. He was smiling, Dan remembered, but he hesitated. There was no reason to be reluctant to include the detail, but most of the time these guys moved in and out of counties and finally states, just passing through. But when Fay stopped taking odd carpentry jobs and took a job full-time with the railroad less than two weeks later, Dan took closer notice.

It turned out Dicey Edwards, Ellis's grieving widow, came into a lot of C&O's insurance money after the killing. State police worked the case for just over a year from afar, watching Mullins show up for work every day, taking notes on Dicey's shopping habits. A new Chrysler appeared in her driveway, she bought clothes from Penny's instead of her usual purchases of Kmart bluelight specials. The case was right under their noses, but Post 9 spent a year awaiting DNA results, awaiting court orders, awaiting the system and working with the county prosecutor, trying to build a case. All this until the Post was finally told there wasn't enough evidence. No witnesses, none who would talk or could remember clearly enough to be helpful, the DNA was shaky. Everybody at Jensen's that night seemed to have danced or groped each other at one point or another. And most importantly—no weapon.

It seemed just when the state police placed Ellis Edwards in the cold case files, there was another murder, this one out in the little hamlet of Rowdy in Perry County. Dan only heard about this one, but it was the closest they came to getting Mullins. His blood and the woman's blood were found on a 1982 Harley left in the parking lot of Newsome's Furniture along Route 23. Mullins' prints were found on the motorcycle. His blood and the victim's blood were found both on the motorcycle and in the abandoned field in Rowdy where she was discovered.

The victim was an out of state woman from West Virginia named Tiffany Jones. Troopers and detectives working her death and trying to tie Mullins in said the photographs were worse than a horror movie. Eyes gouged out, breasts cut off in the same jagged way as the ear-to-ear cut that finished off Ellis Edwards.

"Fay Mullins is an Irish prick killer and a ghost on top of that," Hen said. Stan stared at a spot about three feet in front of him in the bare floor.

Dan stood and absently adjusted his weapon, a habit, a nervous thing he'd done since starting at the sheriff's department when everything went belly up with the family business. He'd never been entirely comfortable with the gun on his side. The first time he'd fired a gun was during his training. Dan stood there and closed his eyes, thought of fresh produce and cash registers and breaking down boxes and ordering supplies.

"You still with us?" It was Stan. The room was smaller with Stan Collins two feet away and standing.

Dan took his hand from his service weapon. "Your brother's missing and Brown Bottle can't be found. I came as a courtesy. We only know that Fay is out in daylight, and that's usually a bad sign." He nodded and started to the door, stopped when Stan started to speak, interrupting him with the turn of his shoulder. "Do what you want, and I'll do what I can. Can't speak for Post 9. You have a good one."

And he was out the door, walking easily and without urgency to his cruiser. Hen crossed her arms and Stan came up behind her. It was a strange thing to see Hen upset beyond simple aggravation. She was doing a bad job of trying to hide it, maybe wasn't trying at all. But she had been doing well until Dan mentioned Fay Mullins. That name made anyone get sketchy with their nerves.

"Can't fool me and you know it. I can tell you're worried, Hen."

"Yep. But I ain't told you exactly why just yet."

13

Tuck examined the knots around his wrists again. Braided rope, knots big as green apples, and the same around his ankles. Military-trained knots, his best guess. His shoulder hurt in a hellfire way, but it was wrapped with what looked to be an old shirt or jacket. He shifted his body as best as possible in the corner of the cabin, plopped as he was there with the spiders and the kudzu growing through cracks in the wall.

That he was here at all was nothing short of amazing to Tuck.

By the best figuring he could manage, it seemed Brown had been gone about twenty minutes, but that could just as easily have been two hours. Tuck pretended to still be out from the pain when he left. Brown had packed a few things in a faded bag, dipped some of that hot whiskey from the washtub and glanced back at him once before he slammed out of the door. He took his gun. That was the clearest thing Tuck remembered.

Tuck would never admit it, but Brown Bottle scared him. If anyone who had ever laughed Brown off were to see Tuck right this second on the floor of a cabin bound like a hog and bleeding, they'd have it to rethink their views. He knew now what all of them would do well to know soon. It's all fun and games until the little dog bites back.

Even after Brown came home from overseas, when he was still Wade to everyone, all of them joked at him, prodded him. They made fun of his haircut, how he wore his dress uniform around just about every day. Tuck joined in, but he knew Brown wore that military dress uniform most of the time because it was the newest clothes he owned. Yet acting that way did Brown no favors, and after a couple years when the television news started telling about how boys from the states had gone crazy overseas and killed babies and all the rest, without a judge or a jury, without so much as one damn question, everybody who had been making fun of Brown's clothes started getting meaner. It was a thousand wonders he didn't end up with the nickname Baby Killer. The more he saw it go on, and the more Brown drank, the more Tuck secretly thought to himself that if he were Brown, he'd be drinking, too. Probably worse. What scared him more than anything about Brown was the fact that he was still here in Sandy. He didn't move away. He took a load of shit, was still taking a load of shit, and was still here. *By God, there's something to it that demanded respect at the very least. And fear if you're smart.*

Tuck pulled again at his bindings, pulled until he was out of breath and settled onto the dusty cabin floor again. Nothing but his mind and the heat and whatever critters wanted to crawl in there with him. He tried his memory for more than that image of Brown walking out the door with the gun, more than the pain of getting winged in the shoulder, when he heard something moving outside the cabin. *A heavy something, not something moving easy through the woods. Something careless, or calm.*

The old mining road was grown over even for fall weather as Nick made his way along it with some care. It started at the mouth of Major Hollow, really, even though some houses dotted the road until the blacktop stopped and turned into the tire-sunken dirt about a hundred feet from Major Dennison's house. Major was his given Christian name, not an honorary title, but nobody cared. Least of all Nick, waving through the tangle vine and wading kudzu as he charted his way eastward up the mountain to his uncle's old cabin.

When Nick made it to the area he and the boys once called White Mountain because of the strange white colors of the trees and plants in that particular part of the valley, he sat to rest. His hands shook, his mouth became dry as a corn husk, and every branch that snapped sent ripples across his muscles. It was the need for nerve pills working on him. He took three Xanax from his shirt pocket and chewed them slowly, hated himself, waited for the wildlife sounds to ease off his nerves. It wasn't a wafer, but it might do. He tongued any clumps lodged into his molars and swallowed hard. When he felt he could stand without a constant urge to slump forward, he raised and waved to the White Mountain valley like it was another old friend who wouldn't say a word to him now.

It was a person, a man, moving outside the cabin. Tuck was sure of it. *And if it's a man, it's Brown. Has to be.* He readied himself by pushing up the cabin wall and standing as straight as possible.

Nick opened the door slowly and entered. The sound of Tuck's breath leaving him in a gust of relief was loud in the single room. Tuck began speaking to him, but Nick crossed the room, looking only at Tuck once, then sat down. Still Tuck went on and on.

"Thank holy God, you're here," Tuck said again. "That uncle of yours is planning on filing me away in a deep mine somewhere, ain't no doubt about it. Thank the merciful Lord, you're here."

"Shut up," Nick said.

"I got stuff I can give you. Free, no pay, no strings," said Tuck. "Just help me get out of here. Brown'll think I worked my way out on my own."

For the second time Nick looked at Tuck, glanced at his bindings. He knew those knots. Sailor knots. A bear couldn't break those. He smiled.

"You think this is funny? You think this is some kind of goddamn whatever! A game!"

Nick sat back down and continued smiling. Uncle Wade showed him those knots years ago in their field, and still he remembered them. It was a fine and good feeling, and a hundred drug dealers screaming like scared hens couldn't shake that from him.

"What do I think? Well, now, let's see. I think my uncle aims to get you good," Nick said. "And it's because of me, because he reckons I get dope from you, even though I really get it from Hen, who mostly gets it, you guessed it, from you. But in the end, it's because I came an ace of dying there in your shithole trailer from getting too damn high."

Tuck lunged forward, torso first, and landed hard to the floor. Dust snowed down from above and the old cabin moved off and back onto the ground like a rib hinging from a deep breath. He gasped and rolled himself over and twisted so he could look Nick in the eye.

"Why don't you do it, you pillhead shit? Go on out there and get a good sized rock and bash my head in?" Tuck stopped and laughed. "It's awful I forced them pills down your throat and up your nose. Poor little boy. Poor little Nick Taylor. You little shit bastard."

Nick smiled and smiled. He stood up and stretched out his arms. Bored. Tired. Done with this episode. In a powder flash he was on the floor, on his hands and knees, his face inches from Tuck's. He could feel the Xanax fully now, easing him out, flattening him to that easy calm.

"I'm not gonna let Uncle Wade rip your guts out, seeing as that's exactly what he'd do if you pushed him to it," he said. "I've done got a guy on you. And that guy, well, he'll bring a lot more than just killing you."

Tuck made exaggerated movements to regain on upright position, hands and feet bound, standing like a tottering plaything for babies. All the signs of being as much of a badass as he could were there, with the exception of his eyes. The color seemed to drain out of them by the second, replaced with a wetness, and a far-off look. The look of a man slow to figuring things out, but always doing so, eventually. A man didn't get into the running business without some sense, even if it was just a four-cylinder without much take off power.

"You're after the money and drugs and since Brown's done after me, you figure knocking me off in the meantime would be the best way to get it all wrapped up in a bow." Tuck said. "I thought Brown was dumb, but my god you take it, Nick. You take it all. Who do you think they're going to take in for killing me? They'll take Brown, you stupid shit."

Tuck had a point in some ways. There weren't a great deal of reasons to have Fay Mullins leave him in an abandoned deep somewhere if he was going to probably be killed anyway. Nick thought of it as insurance, though, and since Ashley was in with him on the plan from the word go, Nick knew it was the best thing to do. *The most comprehensive*, as his science teacher used to say. He had always liked that word after that.

It seemed wise. It was the kind of word, before hearing, he always wanted to call the old men sitting on the porches of their nice homes with their retirement checks coming in and people like him mowing their yards and power washing the sides of their two-door garages. *Those old guys are comprehensive. They got it figured out.*

Besides, he wasn't sure his uncle would pull through with his vengeance. He was dangerous, but a little along in years and not as sharp as before. Besides that—and he wasn't about to share this thought—he didn't figure his uncle for killing anybody, not really. Fay Mullins, on the other hand, had never stopped, and was sharp as a tack, reliable, and would be gone for at least a year and a half after it was all said and done. *Won't have to see his face again, maybe.* That first night after things were locked in with Fay, when Nick was quietly unsure and openly nervous about the entire plan, Ashley reeled him in, became the strong one in that moment when it was needed.

She explained that even though Brown had his eye on Tuck and Stan, the law, including her dad, would hear of Fay being in town and start looking in that direction when Tuck turned up dead and robbed. Said it would likely be figured by the law that another dealer hired up Fay for the job. Still, it all seemed more involved than it needed to be, but the wheels were already in motion. If he had it to do over, Nick would have taken the money and drugs and realized that no one could have picked from the dozens and dozens of drug addicts who might have robbed Tuck.

For now, though, the plan was here, with Tuck mouthing off.

"Dumb's better than dead," Nick said. He stood, pulled his shoulders back. "I have things to do. Don't worry, you'll have a lot of company soon."

A half dozen ideas or images of ideas about how he would deal with Nick went like a slideshow through Tuck's mind, how he might be able to deal with this if he saw the other side of it without harm. *There would be a beating. Of that there was no doubt, Brown or no Brown.* But that anger bloomed only briefly. His arms ached, he could feel dirt pushing into his wound, could hear flies buzzing him. And he still had Brown to deal with when he returned, which was surely soon. The truth was simple. He wanted to plead again like he had from the start. Pride and fear and instinct kept him from it. Instead he could only watch Nick step out the door, holding his tongue while scattered flecks of dust floated from the ceiling and landed like infantrymen all around him.

14

"What ain't you telling me?" Stan asked.

Hen sat on their bed playing with the frayed corners of a wedding ring patterned quilt. Her grandmother made it when Hen told her family she was planning to marry Stan. The name had passed around the kitchen table the evening she told the news. *Stanley Collins? Stanley Collins. Stan Collins?* Every time she heard Stan's name said aloud that night, she felt a tingle go along her forearms. It might have been more lust than love at first, but it would have been a close call. *Stan was never much to look at. Not ugly, just average. Most everything about him was about average, except his heart and his stubbornness.* But she had liked from the very start how he put himself into his work. His labor was like an intense emotion spreading out across a room, thick and powerful and with perfectly aligned direction. Her grandmother told her that night while starting the wedding ring quilt that how a man went at his work was a good sign of how he would love a woman, from the chapel to the bedroom.

Stan walked around the foot of the bed, stood with his arm tucked into his side. When Hen didn't answer right away, he circled back to stand in front of her.

"Give me a minute to figure out the best way to explain," she said.

Stan knew this game from Hen. She had been playing it as long as they had been married. She was cooking up some kind of story right now. He was sure if he was quiet enough he would very nearly be able to hear her brain snapping and ticking away inside her head.

"Just come out with it," he said.

Hen adjusted herself on the bed, stopped plucking at the frayed corner, and patted the spot beside her. Stan took his hand off his hip and put both hands in the air and let out a long sigh before sitting down with her. When he looked directly in her eyes, he saw it. *Fear.* Stan hadn't seen her afraid, truly afraid, in years. Not since she was convinced a lump in her breast was cancer. Only when she got to a doctor who told her it wasn't cancerous did that same look of fear in her eyes fade out.

It seemed for a moment Hen wasn't going to speak at all, but then she said, "So the thing is, Dip, we need money. I'm not trying to make you feel like less of a man or nothing. I promise, but we have to have more money. That's how it started."

It was true. Stan had been more or less forced to sign up for disability benefits a few years back. He missed work more than he made doing it, and the coal company finally fired him. The operator of the mine sat him down in the rundown single-wide trailer set up at the mine for when the owner or another of the higher ups had to stay overnight. They sat in what Stan figured then must have been some kind of eating nook and the operator was smiling nervously when he said that this wasn't something *they* were doing to him, but that it was something *he* had done to himself, leaving them no choice.

He turned to Hen, placing his hand on her shoulder, and asked softly, "How what started?"

"Well, the stuff with the pills and dope," she said. Her head was hanging low now, her chin nearly resting on her collarbone. "I been selling some here and there, baby."

She became a fragile thing at that moment. Not a tear glistened in her eyes, though. Still afraid, she clenched her teeth and tight muscles at the top of upper jaw became like marbles squirming under the skin.

Stan stood up and shoved his hands in the pockets of his blue jeans, started to walk away, and turned back to Hen. It would be only temporary, the feeling he would get from slapping the determination off her face, and watching her breakdown. Part of him wanted to kill her stone dead right where she sat for having anything to do with Tuck and the drugs. The other part of him wanted to kill himself stone dead for putting her in a spot where she was willing to do such a thing for money.

"Christ almighty," he said. "Why would you, though? I could have got some work from somebody paying cash." Hen had always paid the bills and kept up with the banking. Being in the dark had always been something Stan was fine with, but this was the downside of not being involved with the cash flow. "How am I supposed to fix a problem if I don't know how bad it is?"

Hen looked at him and then back at the floor. They could never argue without making it personal, without searching endlessly for who was at fault.

"Well, go on ahead and tell me how this happened, where we're at with it," he said. "Catch me up so I can at least figure out what to do about it now."

Without moving from the bed or raising her eyes to meet his, Hen began to explain how she would sit on the porch month after month and watch the vehicles coming and going from Tuck's place. It was hard, she told him, to watch all that money rolling over at Tuck's and then to step back into their old house and have to fix soup beans and corn for supper the third time that week.

"So the whole thing just got me to thinking," she said. "Thing is, by law his trailer is sitting on your land. Your folks gave the house and the land, the garden, to you. My first thought wasn't to sell drugs, honey.

I went down there to tell him to pay rent. I mean, he's got the money to do it. And we needed the money."

That day, the day she'd had enough of watching the line of traffic all looking like crisp hundred dollar bills to her mind, it was hot, middle of August. Maybe that had been the problem, the thing that caused her to lose her good sense: the heat. By the time she had made it to the front door of Tuck's trailer, she was coated in sweat, her shirt plastered against her back and stomach. She could feel the hairs on her head jumping wildly around in the heat when Tuck opened the door and a blast of cool air pushed its way out of the trailer from the heating and cooling unit installed the summer before. Tuck had actually been holding a handful of money when he answered. While saying hello he had actually started peeling off bills and smoothing them out with his fingers fixed like scissor blades. It might have been seeing the money or Tuck's stupid grin or maybe even feeling that cold rush of air from inside the trailer while their house boiled up on the hill with only the one window unit in the bedroom so at least when they slept they didn't sweat. It might have been any one of those things, but it led her to asking if she could step in and cool down. She had sat down in the cleaner of the two recliners, tried to ignore the smell of moldy food coming from the kitchen sink, and kicked off her flip-flops. She wiggled her toes and noticed Tuck watching them and from there moving his eyes along her foot and leg. Tuck always had a thing for her, but he never approached her, and never looked at her the way he looked at her that day in front of Stan.

Hen looked at Stan now and saw his age in full light. The sag of skin and fat along his jawline, the crow's feet spiking out from the corners of his eyes. She had aged him just the same as time itself. She had aged likely a good decade and a half in the last ten minutes.

"I don't know what happened," she said. "It was hot. I stepped in that stupid cool trailer. Tuck had this wad of money he was counting. I guess the easiness of it just got to me, baby."

Stan picked up a bottle of aspirin on his nightstand beside the bed and shook out two, and dry swallowed them. "My god. My good god. Well, how did that go? Not well, obviously, since you're here telling me now that you're selling drugs." He smiled and shook his head, said it again, emphasizing each word. "You. Are. Selling. Drugs."

"So you see now why this Fay Mullins business is bothering me more than some?"

"Yes," he said, all pain and smiling. "I see exactly."

The two of them sat at the kitchen table with the weak fall sunlight striping the table top. They hadn't said a word in more than five minutes. Hen made scrambled eggs and toast despite it being well after morning.

She knew Stan could eat breakfast three times a day without complaint. Once the food was gone, though, the room was left in a deep silence doing neither of them any good.

"Tell me when you did it," Stan said.

"Did what?"

"First went down there and got started up with Tuck in the drug selling business," he said. "I want to hear it."

Hen imagined how cool it had felt all throughout Tuck's trailer that past summer. It was so relaxing it almost made up for the stink of food stuck to dishes and the cat piss carpet and the dozen other scents held inside there. It was enough to lull her into the trailer and let her guard down.

"What do we do now?" Hen asked.

"It's not what we're going to do, it's what we ain't going to do," Stan said. "We sit tight right here, right here at home. We go about our business, excluding, of course, any drug selling business, Christ almighty." Stan smacked the top of the table and then took in a long, slow breath. "We do things as normal."

Hen's chin was strong, but she pulled at her fingernails, kept placing one hand atop another to keep them from going to her hair where she would normally pull loose a thick strand of hair to curl around her finger.

"Just try to relax, Hen," Stan said. He hated to see her worrying, even if there was every reason to, considering. He got up from the table and walked to the back door that looked down on the garden and the small hill leading up to their house. "Whatever you've got on you, here at the house or elsewhere, we have to get rid of it. I'll deal with Tuck whenever he decides to come home. My opinion, he's hiding out somewhere. Probably has the same information we've got at this point and he's laying low."

A thought occurred to Stan. He turned around and asked Hen to look at him. When she turned in her chair, he smiled. "How much drug money you holding right now?" he asked. "Just tell me and let's be done with it. That money might come in handy should we have to negotiate our safety."

Hen looked to the floor. He wanted nothing more than to step across to her then and hold her tiny body as close to him as possible. It was true, as things stood he now had not only Brown Bottle to worry about, but Fay Mullins, too. And Fay made three of Brown in the category of fit for hell bad.

"I'm stepping out to the garden for a bit," he said. "When I get back, have whatever money and drugs or whatever fixed neatly on this here kitchen table. Once that's done, I'll get up with Tucker. We hand every item on the table back to him and be done with that. Then it's a matter of dealing with Brown."

Stan resisted again the urge to step to Hen and hug her. She needed order right now, not affection, no matter how badly he needed it himself. He stepped outside and let the fall air coming down from the ridge ease its way into his lungs, filling them up with at least some sense of what was normal and expected. Things could get worse, but for now, he couldn't imagine exactly how.

Outside, the garden wasn't much better in keeping Tuck far from his mind. Stan worried for Hen, but somehow he knew he could make things right by her. He always had. Tuck was a different story entirely.

Everything he looked at on the property, in the old homeplace, brought their childhood to his mind. The shack at the far west point of the property was a memory of him and Tuck drinking a Mason jar of stolen moonshine. It was a summer night, the kind that can become perfect from the stars in the sky to the blades of grass around your feet. The two of them barely made it through a few drinks of the shine, but that didn't matter. The rooftop of the shack was another world for them. From the top, they could see the light on in the living room of the house, meaning their mother was still awake, reading the bible as she always did of the evenings. All other windows in the house were dark, meaning their father had retired for the night. It was a time that felt safe, even though they were getting drunk right there at their own home.

It was the first time Stan could remember feeling at peace. His and Tuck's childhood held little to be labeled peaceful until that night. That night was a revelation. Drinking at home, right under their parent's nose, was not only something akin to a high in and of itself, but it became their own safe place. Even when they were both out of high school, the two of them occasionally went to the shack, climbed to the roof, and drank.

Making his way to what was left of the tool shack, Stan stopped in mid-stride and put his fingers to the sides of his head. The aspirin had kicked in, done what it came to do, and was gone now, leaving him with a worse headache than before. While closing his eyes, he saw Tuck, not more than two years out of high school, standing at the door of the shack smiling. It had been the night of the district basketball championship and Tuck had just come from the stadium in downtown Portville. His grin was so wide, Stan knew he was already into a bottle, maybe something else.

With a prideful flourish, Tuck pulled two pounds of weed from inside his jacket pocket, explaining how it all worked. He had secured what he called a front, which meant, he explained, that you give a guy a pound and then they give you the money two weeks later. Small timers didn't have the cash to pay for product up front. Soon he would have the money to get product without paying up front, but he would still have to convince his friends in on the deals to sell a pound. Tuck kept saying *product* with that same flourish he used when he first pulled out the weed.

Tuck tried to keep Stan in the know about the operation, even while Stan, realizing his little brother was intent on going illegal, kept trying to make a case for continuing the small running of moonshine their father had kept up for more than twenty years. It was a safe bet. He even sold a bottle or two a month to the county judge-executive. But Tuck was having nothing of it. Kept explaining how it all worked. He detailed his first big move, sending more than three grand worth of weed by mail with no guarantee that it would sell on the other end. But it only had to be something that wrecked the nerves that way for a short time, and he was willing to take the risk.

There was no talking Tuck down. He had already sold just over two hundred worth at the basketball game. The groundwork was being laid. Stan declined having anything to do with the weed but swore he wouldn't say anything to their mother or father. He could remember clearly telling him that they'd both just steer clear of the other's business. *Hear no evil, see no evil, and damn sure speak no evil.*

By the time Stan made it to the old tool shack, dusk was settling over Garden Road. He fumbled with the rusted lock on the side door and it finally gave, falling into two pieces in his hands. Though there was only the hint of sunlight, he felt around and found his way to the old vice his father had installed for welding. There were still three chairs positioned in a small circle around the vice. To the left of that was the wood burning stove, its front still hanging open, a small pile of rotted stove wood in the floor lay beside.

He and Tuck used to sneak out to the shack in the years before their father retired to watch the men play cards. Over the years, they were invited in to sit and play with the others, talk about the weather and what was going on at the courthouse, who was getting voted in and who was hitting the road. They played low stakes games of Omaha and seven card, cleaned fish of the summer, and made the shack almost as much of a home as the old homeplace.

Standing now in the torn out guts of that place brought Stan down worse than ever. He made a mental note to tear the shack down come summer and put up something else entirely in its place. Maybe an above ground swimming pool for kids in the bottom. It wasn't something natural to him, grieving times past, a more simple life. He looked forward, always forward.

But there was no moving forward with all this mess. Against his better judgment, the play right now was to let things come to them, try to keep Hen feeling as safe as possible. And, as always, be ready. Forever ready.

It was fully dark when Stan eased back in through the front door. He let go the storm door carefully so it didn't bang throughout the house to wake up Hen, that is if she could be blessed enough to find a little rest. She had left the television on the news. On the coffee table was one of their old ashtrays, the thick green glass kind from back when the two of them smoked. Fay had pressed four cigarettes out in the ashtray, each half smoked. Stan looked in the kitchen sink for any glasses smelling of liquor. The sink was empty, but he knew this was the next step if she'd already brought out the cigarette stash.

It wasn't a bad idea, if all the cards were now on the table. He went to the guest bathroom and fished out a half pint of vodka from the under the sink, behind the bottles of shampoo and boxes of Irish Spring soap. He twisted the cap and held the bottle to his nose. He salivated in that stinging way that can happen along both sides of the jaws, just beneath his ear lobes. He turned off the bathroom light and, walking more cautiously than before, made his way to the refrigerator. Inside were two bottles of Ale-8. He took one and popped it open on the cabinet handle so that the hiss peeled out into the kitchen slowly. With a chaser in hand, he took a large slug of the vodka and followed it with a big drink of the Ale-8. It burned his throat but warmed his stomach.

The kitchen table, the old green ashtray, the shack, the pictures on the walls, the memories. It was all more than he could reasonably handle, so checking out with some vodka was the play for now.

Hen was curled into a tight ball in the bed. She always slept more toward the middle of the bed, curled in this way against his back. In place of him, she had arranged two thick pillows behind her. Stan saw her pack of cigarettes on the nightstand and pulled one loose, fumbled in the dark until he found a pack of matches near the lamp, and returned to the living room. He sat in his recliner where the outside light shined in enough for him to strike one of the matches. He took a long draw from the cigarette and, leaning out of the recliner, brought the green ashtray from the coffee table and rested it on his knee. Tuck would be home soon. He'd been gone this long before. Trips to Florida when some of his road agents couldn't make it to get more pills, for instance. Probably what was going on now. All the same, if he was still gone in the morning, Stan would ask around. That's all, just send out small beacons around town, mention of his brother at the gas station, while standing in line at the post office, at the courthouse. Send his feelers out and see what came from it.

The cigarette did his lungs no favors. He coughed and brought up a large amount of congestion from his chest. He rose and spit into the tiny trash can he kept beside the recliner. Hen had made him start using the trash can instead of leaving empty tins of potted meat and pop cans all around the living room. When he leaned back, he saw a set of headlights pull into Tuck's driveway.

His first thought was of Fay. But then he realized it could be someone dropping Brown Bottle off for about the same reasons. *As if one of them ain't bad enough*, Stan thought, and went to the front door, eased it open, and stepped lightly on the front porch.

The streetlight was bright enough so that Stan could see the vehicle without problem. One of those souped up Honda's everybody went wild over a couple summers back, the ones kids would lower so much they couldn't make it across a railroad crossing without sending sparks flying and tearing everything underneath them out in the process.

Two people got out of the car, but there wasn't much he could tell in the darkness. The streetlight sent a deep shadow across the area where they stood. Finally, one of them went to the window at the trailer end facing Stan's house. When Stan saw the figure start jimmying the window around, he darted through the house and retrieved his shotgun, and stepped onto the porch. He knew it would wake Hen, but he fired a warning shot in the direction of the garden's far northern corner.

The two figures froze for an instance and then ran to the car. He could see them better then, a lanky boy and a girl wearing an oversized jacket and cut off jean shorts. Just some tweakers or pillheads, or both. Still, that's the first time he'd seen anyone try to break into his brother's trailer.

The screen door slammed open behind him. "Who'd you kill?"

"Nobody," he said. "Somebody snooping around Tuck's place is all. Sorry. Go on back to bed and I'll be there directly."

"Was it Brown? If it was Brown, you have my permission to shoot him dead. Or Fay. Either one. Hell, pick one." Stan grinned in the dark. *She's incredibly cute when she's sleepy. Even more so when she's angry.*

Hen turned without another word and was back inside the house before Stan made it onto the porch. He put the shotgun in the corner beside the television and then remembered the half pint of vodka he'd left in the recliner when he's stood up. He found it, unscrewed the cap, and took a long drink straight with no Ale-8 chaser. It burned going down, but he knew he'd be asleep soon with a hard buzz going.

Tomorrow he'd head into town, see if he could get a read on where Tucker was keeping himself, see if he could get word to him that his big brother was tired of keeping watch over him day and night. He wouldn't mention anything about Hen and the drugs. That conversation would need to take place face to face, knuckle to knuckle, if he was a guessing man.

15

Brown walked slowly through the library parking lot. Part of him wanted Blair to notice him through the large glass doors in the front, come out and say hello, save him the nerves of going in first. He felt mean thinking this, but Blair was just homely enough to maybe be interested in him. She surely seemed interested in helping him get Mary's address. Awfully helpful. It was worth a mostly cold shower and his church outfit to find out.

There was a lot for Brown to think about in the past couple weeks. But since his head kept returning to Blair, he figured a little time away from worrying might do him some good, keep his mind off drinking, off Nick, off everything. His persistent heart thought it might give him some reason Now, here at the library, at the moment of truth, he kept walking slowly until he stood behind the library staring at the river.

A moment before he let loose the top button of his shirt and sat on the bank of the river when Brown thought he might actually walk in and smile and wave to Blair and approach the counter and say something nice to her. Watching the muddy water rush past, he played in his head the many things he might say. *Might* say, because it wasn't too late. He could still walk through those glass doors, smile and try. He could still move the world on its axis. Right. He could still be standing wide-eyed at ground zero.

Brown focused on the birds snipping and dive-bombing each other. He took the pint of vodka from his jacket pocket and sat it beside the can of Pepsi beside him. He opened the Pepsi and then twisted the cap on the vodka, a ritual, all part of the exact methods of pre-intoxication. Taking a small sip of the Pepsi, Brown held it in his mouth and followed it with a long pull from the pint, taking out the neck and half an inch of the bottle. He did this one more time and then twisted the pint cap back on.

He didn't hear when the back door of the library suctioned open. But at that moment he decided to leave, tucked the pint back into his pocket, got up, turned and there she was, Blair. Short, a bit stubby, and dressed conservatively, shy, feeling less than acceptable.

"Hi, Wade," she said and held up her hand, giving it a small wiggle in the air. "What're you doing out back here?"

The vodka had warmed his stomach some, titled his balance enough that he recovered easy enough from his surprise. "I don't really know," he said. "Sometimes I like to come back here and watch the river."

"And have a little drink?" she said. "Nothing wrong with that, right?"

She walked down the hill to where Brown stood and fussed with the back of her dress before taking a seat on the ground. She patted the space beside her and Brown sat. He took the pint out and looked sheepishly at Blair. He went through his sip and hold and chase routine then tipped the bottle to her. She shook her head.

"Makes me sick is all," she said. "Otherwise, I would surely like to relax a little. You go right ahead. Let's watch the river together. That'll be relaxing enough for me for a lunch break."

Brown noticed she didn't have any lunch with her, but thought not to mention his noticing. The two of them sat in the quiet for several minutes while the river ran past. Brown finished the pint during this time, began hearing the many different things he might say and slowly pushed them away. *Better to remain silent*, he thought.

"Even when muddy, the river is beautiful ain't it," Blair said finally.

"It sure is," Brown said. "Beautiful like you."

Blair snapped her head around and Brown looked down, studied the grass at their feet like a math problem. When he dared to look up, Blair offered a wide smile. He breathed easily, thought about putting his arm around and realized that was probably the vodka prodding him to move too quickly. Instead, he turned his attention back to the river.

The two of them sat like that for another twenty minutes. They spoke a little, of small stuff. As time passed, and Blair finally excused herself to go back to work, Brown felt a huge guilt move over his heart. Blair wasn't homely. She was beautiful. And he had told her that. No matter what else happened in the future, he had told her that much.

When he got up and began his slow walk across the parking lot, he moved just a bit more lightly, not exactly floating, but not exactly burdened from head to toe. There were things to take care of, but maybe, just maybe, there was something waiting on the other side now.

16

The old apartment was the only place Nick had ever known as home. When his mom moved off, he and Brown stayed on, and they took all of her stuff out in boxes and garbage bags and left it at a consignment shop in Portville, taking some of it in trade for a few shirts and a pair of shoes for Nick. The old man who rented them the place still asked only one-fifty a month for rent, just about enough for the two of them to manage together.

It was home, but he hated bringing Ashley there. She was now in the living room sitting on the couch, one of two pieces of furniture in the room, the other being a wooden magazine rack that was there when they moved in. Ashley waited in the living room while Nick walked through the apartment to get a better signal on his cell. She heard him finally get connection and speak briefly to the person he had called Fay, the man who was going to deliver Nick a way out.

She heard him dialing another number. Cracks ran along the walls in the living room. The longer she sat and followed the deep cracks in the wall from the ceiling to the floor, the more depressed she became. She pulled her hair back in a thick black knot and tied it off with a rubber band, then stepped into the kitchen.

She could still hear Nick talking in one of the two bedrooms, but both doors were closed. The kitchen was more depressing than the living room. The refrigerator was an old model, had possibly been sitting in that exact spot for the past thirty or forty years. She opened the refrigerator door half hoping to see full shelves but knowing better.

Inside was a half empty gallon jug of pink lemonade, a box of Slim Jims, and various condiment containers that looked waxen in the weak light. On the bottom shelf sat five jars of pickles, each without lids. Behind those were five or six half pint bottles of cheap whiskey. A person would have to be looking for the vodka to find it. She stood and opened the freezer door. Mostly freezer burn. In the back corner were two ice trays and, besides those, a half empty bag of seasoned fries.

Out the grimed-over kitchen window she looked down on not much of a yard. It couldn't have covered more than ten feet of land before slipping off into a thin excuse for a creek that separated the yard from an expansive field. The field was certainly a house seat at some point in the distant past. Below the window, parts of a car engine were displayed in the grass like chess pieces. Each one was coated in more blackness than the next. Ashley could see Nick studying over these in the sun, his brow turned down and his mouth serious in the way it could become when he straddled something confused. She could see Brown there, too, standing on his skinny legs and rubbing his constant stubble. Nick had told her so much about his uncle she could almost picture how his lost blue eyes searched Nick for the moment when he realized what needed to be done. She grinned and placed her hand flat against the window imagining how Brown would grin, too, covering it with his long fingers, as Nick found the problem and started back to work on the engine part.

Nick still talked quietly in the bedroom, so she meandered her way back into the living room and sat on the couch again. Dust plumed up from the cushions. The motes floated across the room on a shaft of light and settled on an old floor model television set. She remembered Nick telling her about the year after his mom left for Ohio when they still had basic cable. He and Brown watched Saturday morning cartoons every week and Atlanta Braves games on TBS some evenings. Bob Horner and Dale Murphy and light blue uniforms. Brown made Nick a Braves cap that first year they were on their own. Took an all-black cap and painted that cursive A on the front with White Out. Ashley could see the two of them, just like before, Brown headache hangover hurting on the couch and Nick on the floor. The two of them watching cartoons turned to full volume on Saturday morning. Nick wearing his A cap backwards and Brown grinning at his jokes. Once Nick said Brown tried to make a stovetop breakfast for them instead of cereal and burned up the stove and a circular section of the ceiling above it as big as three basketballs. Another time he fixed spoiled hamburger meat and nearly hospitalized them both. Nick was quick to tell her that his uncle wasn't drunk when either one of those things happened. It was important for him to make that point.

The whole scene gave Ashley a fierce ache in the center of her chest. Everything her eyes came across spoke to how these two men lived in some kind of world where hardship was the constant, with only these tiny spaces between heartbeats offering some kind of peace. She saw an apartment that housed two men who lived whatever life they could in the confines of that small space because everything else was no good for anyone.

But this life, more than her life at home, was something she could improve on. When she stood beside Nick, it made both of them stronger. She knew this without being told. With Nick there were no more hours of loneliness in a small bedroom surrounded by her eight-year-old self, the stuffed animals, the pink television and phone, the sounds of her parents a million miles away in the other room, her parents whispering threats back and forth. That kind of torment was far worse, and a singular hurt. Whatever might come up with Nick, she was never alone with it. That was her worst fear, being alone inside a bubble made to look normal but was as cancerous as any other personal hell. She would share this hell with Nick and be truly happy, learn to live and rejoice in the space between single shared heartbeats.

"The ball's rolling good." It was Nick from the doorway of the far corner bedroom. He was pale, the bones of his face more prominent than before, his blue eyes more muddy than when they first met, when she would have sworn his eyes glowed. But his mouth was nothing but a smile. "I mean, this guy ain't telling a lot of details, but it's all moving. That's all we care about right, baby? That it's moving. That we'll be moving on along soon, too."

Seeing Nick standing in his triumph, a thought occurred to Ashley.

"What if this tall guy and this girl you were with at Tuck's call this guy up, too?" she asked. "What's to keep this guy from somehow, I don't know. Screwing everybody over?"

"Well, it works like this," Nick said. "He knows on the one hand he's dealing with a couple tweakers, gone beyond saving and liable to do anything without warning. With me, he only has to deal with one person, first of all, and second, I might have a habit, but the habit doesn't all the way have me, yet. From the way he talked, this guy is smart. He's figuring all of that into the equation. That and, for whatever it's worth, he gave me his word. If we cut him in at the beginning on any money we see from Tucks' stash for at least the first month we're selling, plus a big sort of leaving bonus for the contract, he disappears back into wherever he disappears to and we never hear from him again."

Ashley leaned into Nick, sensed how firm he was on all this planning, and could feel the tension in the muscles along his shoulders. She wished he was set on something else, but it was this for the time being. She did have one thought she couldn't get rid of now that things were actually in motion.

"We won't hear from this guy again," she said. "At least until somebody sees fit to pay him to make sure we do."

"Right. And we'll only have to meet him one time before and one time after," he said. "We'll probably meet with him at Carbon Park tomorrow night and then once after it's all done. It will honest to God be simple."

She considered how somebody hiring Fay against them after it was all said and done was a possibility Nick hadn't thought of until she mentioned it. She turned her head to see his expression and found only his easy blue eyes staring back at her, a blue so calm it was nearly vacant. If he'd thought of it, he wasn't worried, so she wasn't either. She took a small breath in their shared space and closed her eyes away from worry for now.

But later that night Ashley lay awake. Her dad was on patrol and her mom was out. The house sat so empty in seemed to be one deep whisper in her ear. The comfort she had felt with Nick holding to her in his apartment earlier was at odds with a story he told her on the way home.

Nick told her about a time before Brown went off to the military, a time when he was younger than Nick, junior high maybe. Brown was seeing a girl named Holly then. Holly Pritchard. Everyone, including Brown, knew Holly because they knew her father, Kent Pritchard. Kent had to go door to door when they let him out of the federal prison in Inez telling neighbors he was a sex offender.

What he didn't have to tell them was that he repeatedly molested and raped his daughter from the time she was three years old until she was seven. Four years of that kind of evil. Then a high profile court case when he was finally arrested followed by five years of rehabilitation and counseling, all this by the time she met Brown in junior high.

By then she knew Brown was aware of her past, just like everyone else in Port County. Not to mention she was twelve years old and had yet to develop the habit of keeping it all inside and to herself. She told Brown. Then she told him her father was being released that year.

Brown had one possession of his father's—a Marlin .22 rifle. The day Holly told him about her father, he asked her to follow him from school to his house, a clapboard setup beside the Eagle's Claw restaurant where the owner once lived. It had been a nice house, but by the time the owner moved out and bought another place and left it to rent, it had seen better days. Brown and Holly sat on the steps of the front porch that evening and were mostly quiet while a sprinkling of rain started up to fill in the silence.

As Holly explained some of the exact things her father did to her, the rain picked up, tapping on overturned buckets in the yard like a host of small drums being beat on by tiny hands. Within seconds after Holly stopped talking, the rain eased up. A low formation of smudged clouds moved across John Attic Ridge to reveal the blue sky and the sun spread across the yard in front of the porch. Brown said later it was as if God himself had told him what he should do for Holly.

Sometimes violence revealed love, so he asked her to wait on him while he disappeared through the front door, crossed the living room where his and Mary's mother sat with her elbows on her knees drinking beer and watching television, and to his bedroom where he kept the Marlin in the corner beside his bed. Before leaving his bedroom he thought to tell his mother he was going hunting in the hills down by the train tunnel, if she asked. But when he crossed in front of the television with the rifle held longways by his side, she barely moved her head to the side and continued to stare at the screen without saying a word.

Holly said her father lived now on Hen Pen Road, an easy walk from Brown's house. When back on the porch, he took a small shovel from the side of the pumphouse and handed it to Holly, telling her to carry it and he would carry the gun, that they should be to Hen Pen in ten minutes, tops.

Nick said he was given the impression when Brown first talked about the evening after school with Holly, the discussion about her father, the rifle, that it may have been the first time he had spoken of it.

The place where Kent Pritchard rented less than a mile into the hollow was more rundown than Brown's. And Holly, who was sent to live with her aunt in Sandy after the trial, had likely no memory of a place so generally foul. There was no house to speak of, only an abandoned school bus. He had fixed squares of cardboard and tops of garbage cans with black electrical tape and patched them over the numerous windows. Near the bumper was a makeshift outhouse made from what looked like little more than four uneven pieces of particle board. Everything was soaked through from the rain—the cardboard in the windows, the compressed particle wood that had started to come away in dark brown chucks at the top and near the bottom. At some point, and for what reason no one could understand, Kent Pritchard had painted the bus, converting it from the faded yellow and black of a bumblebee to a shade of light blue like a sickened skyscape in an industrial city. On the hood sat two empty chicken coops.

Brown and Holly climbed to a ridge overlooking the house and beyond that the nearby Big Sandy River, a muddy fast-winding python close to where they spotted Kent Pritchard in what served as his rain-swollen yard shaping with a hammer something from what looked to be long strips of guardrail. His clothes were drenched through so that his ribs showed beneath his shirt. His hair hung wet into his eyes, and every so often he stopped pulling and yanking and took a long drink from a fifth of brown liquor. Brown told Holly he wished her father was sober for this. When Pritchard went into the bus, Brown started digging the hole in the muddy ground at the top of the ridge, trying to dig through to another place, he said, a place far away from people like Kent Pritchard.

The two of them sat close together on the wet ground until dusk began to settle over the hollow, a soft collection of purple lights among the dying clouds. Brown worried he would lose the light and the hole would have to wait open to the rain for another day. When Kent Pritchard slammed the doors of the bus open and lurched out into the yard, he heard Holly take a deep breath and hold it. She pushed herself up onto her hands and edged closer to Brown.

Before sitting the rifle in, Brown said he remembered a pack of Teaberry chewing gum in his shirt pocket, pulled a piece out, and handed it to Holly. It was the kind of thing a twelve year old would do, he would say years later, a gesture of the innocent, of kindness and soothing. He spoke to her in a whisper and adjusted the stock against his thin shoulder. It was the first time, he told Nick, he had looked down the barrel of a gun at anything. Up to that point he had not so much as took aim at a squirrel. Now this man, this destroyer of children, of Holly, stood unsteady in his sites. He could see the patches of beard along his jaw line, like rat hair pasted to his skin. The clanging of the metal made for an off-beat drum roll across the mountains. Brown used it for a countdown.

Ten, nine, eight. Pritchard stood from the bent position he had been working and peeled off his shirt. Tattoos, swelled belly. Seven, six, five, four. Back to swinging the metal around the muddy yard, and the purple sky changing to the deep crimson of a rose where it met with the mountain tops in the distance. Three. Two. And one.

Nick hadn't heard anything else about what happened after, except about Holly. Maybe Brown hadn't said. Maybe he hadn't even said anything about Holly. It would have been something Nick would already know. Everybody knew, just the same as everybody knew her father, what he had done. Ashley knew. But they must have dragged the body to the ridge in a streak of blood and rainwater. It would have been fully dark by the time they dropped her father into the opened ground.

Ashley thought of Holly Pritchard and rolled to her side, tried again to sleep. She imagined how Holly must have loved Brown, even at twelve, and how much he must have cared for her, too. The sacrifice he made. She thought of this and whispered what Brown said he had whispered to Holly that day after handing her the pack of Teaberry. She said to the ceiling, "By the time the sweetness is gone, it'll be over." Five minutes later, she knew only the darkness of sleep without dreams.

17

The absence of sound woke her. It would have normally been the sunlight, pouring in the window at what must have been mid-morning, but at this hour the house should have had that electric buzz of her parents, the kind of buzz she always heard in the background, like the current running to a streetlight, unnoticed until it was gone. Ashley stumbled from her bedroom into the long hallway leading to the living room. Still the silence, a late night quiet. In the living room everything still sat where she left it the night before—a copy of *In Touch* on the recliner, her cereal bowl, the milk now hardened along the bottom, a hair brush left in the floor where she had sat, combing and running the evening with Nick through her mind. The harshness of that memory in the daylight gutted her with worry in an instant and she pushed it away.

"Mom? Dad?"

No response. She had a thought and trotted across the kitchen to look out the window above the sink. Her dad's police cruiser and her mom's Camry were both missing from the driveway. She stood at the sink and twirled a long strand of chestnut hair around her finger, picked up the house phone and dialed the sheriff's office.

"Sheriff's office," a female voice said.

"Kathy, it's Ashley. Is my dad there?"

"Sure is honey," she said. "Oh, wait. Gerald's shaking his head. He must've left back out. He was here for an early meeting but they said he peeled out about five minutes ago. Sneaky, that dad of yours. You want I should leave a message?"

"No, that's okay. Thanks."

From time to time her mom would park inside the garage. Ashley slipped on her shoes, grabbed a jacket, and stepped into the fall air. She pulled the side door of the garage open and flipped the light switch. The Camry sat crooked in the middle of the garage, driver's side door swung half open, her mother sleeping in the driver's seat.

Asleep or dead, it could have been either. She had seen her in this way before, pallid, no clear sign of breathing. How had her dad not? She didn't want to cross the five feet of space to the opened door. Instead, she stood in the doorway wiping sleep from her eyes, waiting for a sign of movement from the driver's seat. When her mom gave out a light snore, she knew it wasn't going to happen and went to her, pulled roughly on her arm.

There was no scent of liquor in the car, no skunky aroma of weed. Ashley finally took her under the arm and lifted her to a standing position. She held her there in the middle of the garage until she began standing on her on, at last opening her eyes like two blue dying stars blinking in and out in the night sky.

"Hi, baby," she said.

Ashley turned her face away and moved her first to the doorway and then through the hallway to the living room before easing her in a fold of arms and legs onto the couch.

"Get me some water, baby. I'm dry as a cork."

Pills. Likely hydrocodone of some kind. Ashley had been around enough recreational prescription pill abuse to notice the cottonmouth it created. She took her cell phone and scrolled through, dialed her dad again.

"I'll get you some water, Mom."

"No, orange juice if we have any, okay? Orange juice is the best. Good cold orange juice."

"Okay," she said, listening to the fourth ring and then her dad's short voice message and the tone. "Dad, where are you? Mom's here and it ain't good. She's either high or I'm seeing things. Call me."

She sat on the couch, was about to get settled, and her mother tossed her legs across Ashley's lap. She was a bird-like thing in her prone position, all arms and legs. The left strap of her tank top had fallen to rest just below the bend in of her arm revealing a cream-colored bra. Her lips were plump and red but cracked from dehydration. The natural curls of her hair had converged on one another to form large tangles that stuck to the sides of her head. There were bruises along her shins like misshapen Easter eggs sadly colored and discarded. Soon Ashley joined her in sleep, the orange juice untouched on the coffee table.

It was nearly midday before Ashley woke on the couch. It was clear her father had been there. His gun, badge, and extra clip dotted the kitchen counter the same as always after a shift. She was exhausted with what felt like a constant search party effort since she had woke earlier in the morning. Still, she crossed the kitchen and made her way slowly down the hallway to her parents' bedroom. She was a little surprised to find both her mother and father in bed together.

The quilt hadn't been turned down. Both her mother and father lay still across it. The pillows were thrown into the floor, and both were still dressed. Her father's shoes were off, but otherwise he was still in full uniform. Seeing her mother's slow breathing, the fall of her chest, the pucker of her lips and how she held a breath inside her cheeks as long as possible before exhaling it all at once, depressed her even more. Ashley wondered if her father had found this situation more than once. Was it just an old hat for him, something familiar in way that could break the heart? She stepped quietly into the room and went to her father's side of the bed. She shook his arm at the shoulder and he immediately opened his eyes.

"How'd she get home?" His voice was crisp and alert, though his eyes were bloodshot. A few years working nights had enabled him to be fully ready at a moment's notice.

"I think she drove," Ashley said. "Is she on pills, Dad?"

He moved himself off the bed in slow motion, stood, and put his arm around her. "Let's talk about this later. This ain't for you to worry about just yet. I'll tell you when to get worried. For now, there is a problem, but it's just mine and your mom's problem."

Ashley didn't care for his answer, but hugged to his side. He kissed her on the cheek and the two of them eased from the bedroom and went their own directions throughout the house. She heard the shower and the sound of the water reminded her of rain, reminded her of how tired she was just then. Tired of so much.

There was no way to keep from connecting what she knew was her mother's pill high and Nick's plan to move likely the exact same drugs for profit, all with her help. It caused more than conflict in both her heart and mind. She sat down in the middle of the hallway and finally cried quietly into her hands. She felt how ugly her face was pressed against her palms, twisted and deformed in anguish, split in three places. One for Nick, and one broken and soaked section each for her parents. There was nothing left for her, no time to consider herself inside the swirling thing that was her life. So she did the only thing she knew to do now. Nick had said they would meet Fay sometime tonight. She needed to focus on those details, get in touch with Nick, get what she needed from the house for a stay at Yellow Flats. She called Nick and made sure when she spoke that her voice didn't waver.

18

Dan sat on the back patio in a pair of basketball shorts and nothing else. His hands and feet were wrinkled from staying in the shower too long and his hair stuck wetly to his head. It was warm for a fall afternoon. Even if it hadn't been, he would have stayed on the patio longer than usual.

Lana hadn't moved from the bed. He checked in on her again before putting on a pot of coffee. She might have been dropped from a building and landed in a heap. Once the coffee was finished he poured half a mug and then added milk until it sloshed at the brim. He needed the coffee fast and didn't have time to wait for it to cool.

After gulping it down in four drinks, Dan returned to the bedroom and sat down with all his weight at once on the corner of the bed. The springs creaked and Lana gave out a faint moan, covered her face with her forearm, and then went motionless again.

"Get up," he said. When she didn't move, he said it again, more forcefully. He wanted her to hear the anger in his voice.

All at once, Lana sat up. She propped herself with her arm and ran her fingers through her hair, pulling loose knots and tangles that sent stray strands of it floating away across the room.

"Don't start," she said. "Ashley's somewhere in the house, probably listening at the door right now."

He went to the closet. There had been no plans to get dressed today, he meant to stay in his basketball shorts and forget the world outside existed, watch some old movies, maybe get a little drunk. But dressing gave him something to do, something that might stave off the anger, keep it from blooming so quickly into rage. There was some ground to cover with Lana. He needed to pace himself.

While pulling on a pair of jeans and a polo, he listened to her moving behind him. A clinking of items from the nightstand, a rapid fire pulling open of various drawers, and then a pause. Dan could nearly hear her mind working, a frantic thing, a starving animal scratching at the inside of her skull.

"You're not going to find any pills," he said without looking around. "Unless you plan on cracking open my evidence box out in the trunk of the cruiser. Unless you do that, you can forget it."

He expected an instant fit of screaming. He expected lightning and a bomb-like shaking of the ground, a twisting loose of the foundation. When Lana said nothing, he turned to face her. There was a strange and out of place softness to her features, the half-lidded eyes, a slight pucker in the lips. It made him more anxious than if the room had lit up with all the blinding wrath of heaven.

"What do you expect me to do, Dan? Huh?" She stepped closer to him, met him with her gaze. "Lately you've been absolutely missing in action. Serve this paper, sit in for this trial, sit in for that one. And now there's all this shit with the two drug dealers trying to kill each other and whatever else all of that means."

"It's just one drug dealer, not two," he said, and at once regretted it.

"Excuse me," she said. "And congratulations on missing the point entirely."

Then at once, the fact they were discussing drug dealers struck him in the hardest, most direct way possible. She stood condemning him for doing his job to work against a drug dealer, likely the very dealer who, at least at some level if not directly, was providing her with pills. That fact welled up inside him, an emotion that paled simple rage. Dan saw his arm raising and watched his fingers splay out from his palm. It all happened without his permission, the hitting her. When Lana fell back onto the floor, clutching her face, Dan immediately went to her as if the falling had nothing at all to do with him.

The washcloth spread across the left side of her face had lost its chill. Lana stood up slowly from the kitchen counter and went to the sink. She ran it under cold water, squeezed it mostly dry, and then twirled it a few times. It was an old trick her grandmother showed her the first time Ashley had a fever. The cold chill felt good against her stinging cheekbone, so at least there was that to be thankful for.

Within seconds after Dan left for the grocery store, most likely to get beer, she started a full out search through the entire house, but found no pills. How could she not have dropped one or two at some point since bringing her first prescription home?

That first prescription came the day she had her hysterectomy. Perc 10s, forty count. At first she made sure to read the side of the bottle to make sure if she could take a second pill during the day. One by mouth twice a day. Okay, she could have another. By the end of the first week, two a day became four a day, four a day became six a day. At the end of that first month after her surgery, she couldn't get to the pharmacy fast enough. The script had one refill, which meant next month she would have to go back to Dr. Sowards for more.

It went like this until Dr. Sowards denied a third refill, explaining she couldn't possibly still be experiencing pain. Yes, she told him, she absolutely was experiencing pain. Lots of it. In that case, he told her, something must surely be wrong. Rather than refilling another script, he wanted to admit her for examination. She had to get creative then, pleading him off a hospital stay for tests with a flurry of excuses, promising it would be easier a couple weeks from then. She would just have to deal with the pain, somehow, until then. Sowards gave her six Lorcet fives and told her to ration them until she could arrange time for a stay.

In the parking lot after that visit, Lana dry swallowed the six pills before pulling out of her parking space. She sat with the car idling and leaned her head back, closed her eyes, and waited. At home later, still buzzing, but aware the high was nearly worn off, she called Stan Collins. Dan bought corn from Stan most seasons. His number was in their list of contacts on the kitchen counter under S. Dan's clunky handwriting proclaimed SWEET CORN! just beneath Stan's name.

Lana could remember the sound of Stan Collins' voice when she asked for Tucker, the way it fell a notch or two in timber, became slow and worn out, tired, fed up. It reminded her of how wind would take a warm turn just before rain in spring, a quiet, easy ushering in of noise and natural power. He told her shortly that Tucker was in the phone book and hung up.

The conversation with Tucker was even more strained. For the most part he dodged her subtle attempts to ask about buying pills while keeping the possibility ever so slightly at the center of the exchange. By the end of the call, she was pretty sure Tucker had given her three people to contact about making a buy. Either that or he was generally prone to bringing up random names for seemingly no reason.

She had found the three numbers in the phone book and then Jensen Caudill hadn't panned out when she called. He was clearly nervous and rushed her off the call. Her second attempt had been Iree Milam. Much of the same, with a little more confusion than with Jensen. But the third number had been the one.

She took the phone from the charger on the counter, stepped onto the front porch in case Ashley should wander into the kitchen unexpectedly, and dialed the first number she had tried last that first time many months ago. She only hoped Hen picked up and not Stan, who didn't even trust his own brother. Those three had more secrets than a Freemasons' meeting.

Dan regretted changing out of his comfortable clothes. He felt bound up in his jeans and shirt, closed off inside the cab of his truck, suffocated. He rolled the window down, took in a deep breath of fall air, and turned the radio dial to a classic rock station. Remembering a cigarette he stashed under the seat not long after he stopped smoking last summer, he leaned over and plucked around with his fingers until he found it. There was a stash of old lighters in the console. He took one, lit the cigarette, and rolled his window down two inches.

Axl Rose's high, pitch-perfect scream filled the cab as "Welcome to the Jungle" came on the station. Dan turned up the volume and leaned back into his seat. He felt less confined drawing on the cigarette, more at ease in a way he had forgotten could happen. It was as if he was newly graduated from high school again without much to worry about except working for his dad and partying with friends in the evenings. Those days, a trip in a vehicle was about more than getting from point A to point B. The young Dan appreciated the journey, a steady gush of fall air, a good song, no one to piss off or please. It was as close a thing to freedom as he would ever know. *Old Dan likes it pretty good, too*, he thought.

His original intention had been to stop by the grocery store, get whatever was needed for the house and a whole pecan pie for himself, along with a half-gallon of milk. On the way home, the plan was to stop at the foot of Abner Mountain and park to eat the pie and have some milk. But now he was up for more than just stealing some time and calming down. The way he felt, he could drive halfway to the West Coast and take the first hotel room he saw once he got tired. Get back up the next morning and start out again. Music, smokes, a little money, and the road.

It would be nice. There was no denying that. Like everything else these days, Dan knew it was nothing more than a pipe dream, a secret hope he stored away so many years ago he couldn't remember what first started him in that direction to begin with. It was likely a small argument early in the marriage. Something he didn't want to face and so he made this personal plan of escape that would never amount to anything. But it was still nice.

He passed the IGA grocery and tried not to think of the west coast or pecan pie. He tried to let his mind ease back into the reality waiting at home. The reality waiting at the department. He did this and tried to ignore how both lines of reality were beginning to blur, beginning to grow into one life moment that might define him and his family. He tried not to think and he tried not to think and he didn't think. He drove and drove all the way home.

19

Stops always had to be made on the way to finishing a job, and not all those stops had something to do with the target. Fay waited for the last light to blink out in Dan Bell's house and walked across the street.

He knew the cop was gone, but the daughter might still be home with the wife. It didn't matter one way or the other that the daughter was one-half of his client. They were both, her and the boy, the youngest clients he'd ever taken on, and when it was all said and done, how he made it happen wouldn't much be questioned.

The cop, the wife, the daughter. But he knew their names. More than that, he knew their mamaws' and papaws' names. He knew the cop's schedule, even his little pissed-off drives always following an argument. He knew the make of handgun he carried. Issued, in need of cleaning from non-use. The wife, he knew about her, too, of course. That's why he walked in the dark toward her front door with a blade in his hand. They may call elder abuse the quiet crime, but Fay would always and forever make an argument for a well-sharpened Gerber Mark II.

The front door was basic, less than a minute. He eased through and stood a full half-minute to adjust to his settings. Foyer, left looked to be the kitchen. A hallway to either a living room or bedrooms to the right. The only sounds were electronics buzzing low, a ceiling fan somewhere to his left.

All this shit with these two hillbillies at each other's throats and the details from the kids who got their hands on some money enough to hire didn't distract him from the fact that Lana Bell surely wasn't buying from the drug dealer, not these kids' drug dealer anyway. He hadn't seen her coming or going from Tucker Collins' place. She didn't much leave the house, really. Plenty enough visitors during the day, though. Too many to narrow down where the pills or the coke or the meth was coming from well enough without talking to the wife herself. Why get just one drug dealer when you can get two? Why not more money? These were questions that didn't have to settle for long in Fay's mind. At some point, likely after about the third or fourth time a job went sideways and left him with the short stick, the idea of raking in everything he could off the table became his standard. *Blow it all to hell and walk away with the wind and smoke.*

Brown did stick in his craw some, if Fay was being honest. He caught a look at him shortly after the hire. Something about his face, the way he held it firm while the rest of his body stayed relaxed. He'd seen this sort of thing before and it had rarely preceded much of anything good. A drunk was a dangerous sort of person, anyways. Pain registered slower, that old and best weapon fear was dampened. And then on top of this sort of thing, his damn face held hard like that all the time. Held in such a way that made his eyes not so much intimidating as irrelevant, and aware of their irrelevance. Fay would like to have been able to sum up the drunk as a man with wet brain and nothing to lose, but he knew there was more to him. He'd seen dogs with eyes like that, shot dogs and been made to suffer by dogs with those kids of lost eyes. Might be some kind of trouble that would call for careful and clear thought down the line. Not uncharted territory by a long stretch, but standing now in the cop's house with work to do, he didn't like that the drunk was already in his head. He shifted focus, made peace with his mind.

The daughter had left shortly after the cop. *Off to see her young man,* Fay supposed. So wherever the wife was in the house, she was quiet, likely passed out or close. Easy was something he was always thankful for, but if she was too far gone, it could be more difficult to get answers. He eased left and entered the kitchen. On an island in the middle of the room sat a bowl with two browned bananas stuck at the bottom. He picked the bananas out and moved to the sink, turned the water on just enough for a stream the size of a cheap necklace, sat the bowl under it, and waited for it to fill.

He carried the bowl carefully through the living room just off from the kitchen and pushed lightly on the door with his foot. It swung open slowly and, even in the darkness, Fay could see the room was mostly done in pink. *The daughter, the boy's girl.* He backed out, watching the tilt of the water so it didn't slosh over the rim of the bowl, and continued his careful walk through the house to the hallway. One of the bedrooms at the end of that hallway was the wife. He dipped his finger to test the water and wiped it dry on the leg of his pants.

In Ireland, in the North especially, it wasn't uncommon to deal with men who were drunk or worse. And deal with them in all manners imaginable. Information gathering. Torture. General mayhem. These broken humans were found in bars, in alley ways, in flats turned to flophouses for the strung out, the ones who were never made to live in a state of war. Fay always thought these types of men must have dreamed while drunk or high of other places on the island, lands were green hills rolled and pubs trembled with happy songs and city streets saw actual pedestrians walking to actual shops or stopping to have coffee in a bookstore. They must have dreamed of the true heaven, not the heaven people hoped for during mass or while bleeding with a chambered bullet two feet from their temple. Not the place told of in bible verse and thrown around to scare young people away from young mistakes.

These junkies and drunks dreamed in shades of perfection. And they dreamed deeply.

The next bedroom was more brightly lit. A streetlamp shown through a large window above the bed and Fay could see the wife in the bed. She breathed deeply. The quilt lay in a crumpled ball in the floor at the foot of the bed. Fully clothed, she might have been napping. Fay stepped to the side of the bed and held the bowl inches above her face. When he turned it, he turned it quickly and a fair amount went into her open mouth. She sat up scream-choking and ran both hands through her hair several times. When she finally stopped and when her eyes found Fay standing at the side of the bed, Fay grabbed her throat and pushed her flat of her back on the bed. He straddled her, covered her mouth with one hand, pressed his other forearm down onto her chest, and let her kick her legs until she became tired and stopped. She did this four times before stopping entirely. Fay was sure she had not been this tired, this terrified. All was going well so far.

"I worked the railroad for a good while," Fay said and stopped. The wife had slipped out again, eyes rolling, lips going slack. He tapped three gloved fingers against her forehead. "Stay on with me here for a bit, wife. I worked at the railroad for a good while. A man has to stay healthy for that. Has to stay healthy for this work, too."

Fay stood up and clapped his hands against his chest. Lana's head dropped to the side, twisted her neck in an odd way, and snapped back to attention, eyes wide, mouth firmly taped. Fay reached and turned the bedroom light on.

"There, that might be better," he said, and sat beside her on the bed. "Straight and to the point, wife. Where you getting these wonderful, magical, pills, huh? Give us a name and we will go, me and the mouse in my pocket."

He pulled the tape from her mouth in one motion. She screamed, a long, drawn out wail at first that died away to a hoarse rattle. Fay leaned back with an exaggerated look of surprise, leaned back in when Lana took a long draw of breath and started screaming again. He pushed the tape back across her lips.

"Okay, we'll calm down now," Fay said. "My time table's not so bad we can't take a minute here and collect ourselves."

He noticed Lana's eyelids drooping and punched the back of her head, a quick jab, and then lay back, pulling her with him so that the two of them were side by side. He stretched out so that his shoulders gave an audible pop.

"Do you dream when you nod off like that?" he asked. "When you pass out, I mean. I've never had a drink in my life, never snorted a line or swallowed a pill or tapped a vein. It would seem I'd at least have a penchant for the drink, I know, I know. But truth is, I've not chipped the first red brick of this temple, wife."

Fay rolled onto his side into a shaft of artificial light coming from the window. He could see a trickle of blood on the bed sheet. Lana seemed as alert as he'd seen her since walking into the bedroom. He wanted to see her fully alert, needed her to be, but now he wanted that panic again. Fear spurred him forward at times, as it did for most, he supposed.

"I do have one vice, a sin that eats away at me," he said, leaning in far enough to smell deodorant and the heaviness of her sweat clinging inside his nose. "Lust, little wife, that's my weakness."

He groaned and raised his knees, tugged at the front of his pants.

Lana thrust her body up from the bed and swung both legs to the right so that her body shifted off the bed and spilled her onto the floor. Fay allowed her this. He leaned up on his elbow and watched her slump-walk through the doorway and into the hall. He listened to her slam down the hall for a couple seconds and exhaled loudly, raised from the bed in a single bounce.

"Do you dream of the true heaven?" he called out. He sped into the hallway and rushed up behind her just before she tilted and fell into the front foyer. When he grabbed her around the waist, she whined pitifully. "Do you find those magic pills in your dreams?" He asked this in a sing-sing voice into Lana's ear, softly, holding her around the waist, allowing her to flail her arms in circles to land small strikes against the tops of his shoulders. "WHERE DO YOU GET YOUR DRUGS, YOU BITCH?"

Lana's body folded up. Fay could sense her giving in. His throat felt raw and scratched from screaming. He had allowed the peace in his mind to be disrupted. He slowed his breathing and dragged Lana by the arm back into the bedroom. She didn't resist, and collapsed in a clump at the foot of the bed. Fay bent to her, slowly, deliberate.

Fay had filled a second bowl of water, this one hot enough to heat up the metal of the faucet, after taping Lana's mouth. It sat on the dresser and he went now and dipped his finger. Still hot enough to be extremely uncomfortable to the skin. Fay took it in both hands and stepped in front of Lana. When she looked up at him, he tossed it as hard as he could directly into her eyes. He ripped the tape from her mouth again.

Lana fought to speak, her lips pushing the tape outward. Her scolded cheeks shone red and he could see blood splatter again on the bed sheets. Fay watched the tape swell out and back in as if it were a Morning Glory opening and closing.

"You will stop that and let me get my peace of mind back," he said. He twisted her chin around fast, checked the back of her head. There was a knot where the skin had split open to the left of her crown. She continued her screams, though much weaker now. Fay replaced the tape.

"You got skin thin as a grape peel, wife," Fay said, his voice calm.

Everything about him had become calm. He understood himself enough to know at what point he and Lana Bell had reached. He pulled the Gerber from the back of his belt and turned it over in front of Lana's eyes. Fay could see the rush of air from her lungs push the tape outward like a swelled belly. He let this go on for a time until she tired out again and removed the tape. It would be the last time he needed it.

"Hen," she groaned. "Hen Collins is who I get my stuff from."

Fay didn't smile, didn't make light of anything or needle and prod Lana. It had been easy after all. The rest was even more than easy. It was routine, sometimes boring.

20

It was a strange thing to hear nothing at Carbon Park, not so much as crickets or a car moving on the two-lane far across the park. Ashley sat beside Nick on a picnic table under the number three shelter. Shelters one and two had long ago been mostly destroyed. Pillsheads, methheads, drunks, and Oxyheads, among others, with too much time on their hands and anger in their hearts. They had no clue what to do other than break or burn something. The number three wasn't much better. One picnic table left from what started at six, a table that someone had finally decided to place in the middle of the shelter for some kind of balance, it seemed. Across the concrete foundation were patches of various graffiti, hearts with names around them and crooked arrows painted through the middles. There were two places someone had painted the letters NOW and then beneath that New World Order. The fine work of the never sober.

And they were about to add to that population.

Nick took a wadded ball of tin foil from his pocket and began working it open. As it flattened out, he placed it on the picnic table. It held twenty Lortab fives. This is where they'd be moving most of the stash from Tuck's when they had it in hand. Fay Mullins wasn't supposed to be at the park to meet them for another hour and a half. In half an hour, Christy Simpson would pull up in her VW Beetle and join them at the picnic table. Nick would sell her however many Lortabs he could and tell her to spread the word. It was good business. That much he had learned from Tuck, at least.

Ten or fifteen minutes passed and a set of headlights eased from the main road. It was Christy's Beetle. The lights shut off and though Nick and Ashley looked long and hard into the darkness, it took several minutes for the silhouette of a girl to emerge walking from where the car had been parked. It was Christy. She was already high by the looks of it. Her long red hair was nested in several places, her clothes had that smudged look that came from at least a week without a wash, and her face was a wreck, eyeshadow smeared outward in black bursts from her eyes, lipstick gone but for faint streaks beginning at the corners of her mouth and extending to her cheekbones like butterfly wings. She staggered to them on legs thin as two broom handles taped together.

"Big Nick," Christy said. "My big Nick."

She wrapped her arms around Nick, and Ashley was in between them in less than a second. Christy backed up and raised her arms. "Whoa, lady, it's all good. It's just old times and everything."

Nick took a couple steps back. "It ain't old times, Christy."

"Most definitely not," Ashley added, glaring at Nick.

"Okay, okay. Shit. Well, you got some Lorcets?"

"Lortabs," Nick said. "Does it matter? Honestly?"

"I'm picking up on your sarcasm there, buddy," Christy said. She laughed and stretched out on the picnic table. The piece of tin foil with the pills was still in the middle of the table and Christy noticed them. "Oh, yes. Here we go."

Ashley grabbed the foil and wadded it back into a ball, stuffed it into her bra.

"Honey I don't care to go there. We'll make some old times of our own."

"Cut this shit out," Nick said. He stepped between the two of them. "Ten apiece. Two-hundred."

Nick knew he'd overpriced by about double. Oxys would go for around a dollar a milligram, Percocet fives would move at about five. It was all about the milligrams, unless you were lucky enough to get hold of some methadone wafers. Hard as holy hell to get, these went for fifty a wafer. But he hoped Christy was too high to know the difference between tens and fives. He doubted right about now she knew the difference between her hands and her feet.

"Slick Nick. That's your new name," Christy said. She laughed and sat up. Her eyes narrowed and sharpened. "I'm not buying all of them, because I'm not spending all I got right now, which, by the way, is a hundred bucks. Which, by the way, is how much you got resting lucky against your lady's tits over there."

Nick shook his head. "That was long-winded for saying you ain't going to pay double."

Christy shrugged her shoulders. "I'll take five for the road. Maybe the rest tomorrow."

She stood and leaned into Nick again. Nick could remember the old times, and they weren't that bad. Christy had been good in bed before the drugs, back when it was nothing but pot and drinking shots from the bottle. Generous and soft, but aggressive when it called for it. The kind of girl a guy remembered, thought about from time to time. But never with love in his heart. Always lust. Christy was a vehicle for lust. Like its own addiction, she carried it with her to any place she went. It was like an addiction in that way, but instead of sticking to her, lust sprayed out from her, through her pours. Even in her condition, her hair, the makeup, the sores beginning to show on her forehead and cheeks, it was the way she held herself, as if she would fall into you and let you have her in whatever way you needed at any moment, that made Christy an addiction in and of herself.

There had been a low drum of thunder since nightfall, so when Ashley hit Christy in the nose with the base of her hand, Nick first thought lightning had struck. He saw Ashley extend the upward strike high into the air and recalled her telling him about a self-defense move she'd picked up on watching a Quentin Tarantino movie once. If you hit a guy this way, she had said, showing him that same upward hit, it'll break his nose. Maybe even kill him because of how the bones of the nose might move up into the brain. "Do that," she told him, "it's game over."

Christy dropped stiff as cordwood and upended the picnic table. Ashley followed her down and had both fists going before Nick made it to her and pulled her away. She kicked so hard while he pulled her away from the shelter, her flip-flops went flying, one landing on top of the shelter. If she was saying actual words, Nick couldn't have told anyone what they were. They came through with the screams so that it was one long bray.

When all the sounds split and went outward into the night, Nick caught another sound just behind it. A man's voice, out past the baseball field on the far end of the park. Nick hushed all of them.

"It's him," he said. "See?" He pointed toward the baseball field.

"Come on," Ashley said. She grabbed Christy's arm and began walking her to her car. Nick didn't watch them go, but he heard the Beetle start and pull out. By that time, the figure walking across the park was more clearly defined. He recognized the man and hung his head down, stuffed the pills deep into his pocket. When Brown was less than ten feet away, Nick sat and folded his arms.

"I always take a short cut through here," Brown said, shrugged his shoulders, and pointed to Ashley making her way back to the shelter. She gave an awkward wave and Brown gave an equally awkward wave back. "What are you all doing? Nick, bub, are you high or anything? You okay?"

"I'm not high, Uncle Wade. We're just out, you know, hanging out. But we're getting ready to leave."

No sooner was Ashley back to the shelter, Nick motioned to her for them to move along. She nodded to Brown and turned to join Nick.

"Catch up with you later, Uncle Wade."

"Who's that?" Brown asked.

Nick followed to where Brown pointed, near the park's central building. A tall, gaunt man stood with his hands in his pockets. He wore a heavy coat and lifted his hand to wave them over.

"That's him," Nick said.

"Who?" Brown asked.

"Uncle Wade, we have to go talk with this guy. We'll see you later."

"That guy is bad business," Brown said. "What in holy heck are you two doing meeting here in the park at night with a shady guy like that?"

"And that's it for the questions," Nick said. "Ashley, you stay here if Uncle Wade's going to stick around. I'll go over and talk to him."

Ashley turned to Brown and put her hand on his shoulder. He withdrew without looking away from Nick. But Nick was already walking toward Fay, and so Brown allowed Ashley to lead him to the picnic table and sat with her.

"Nick's just getting this guy off our back about some kind of big plan these guys have up around Turnberry to break into all these Mom and Pop grocery stores up through here," she said softly. "Somebody dropped Nick's name to this guy and now Nick's telling him we're not interested. Boom, boom. That's that."

Brown smiled. The stubble along his cheeks folded into deep wrinkles, his lips parted briefly, but his eyes remained unchanged, unmoving from where Nick now stood speaking with Fay.

"Who is that man?" Brown asked.

"I just told you."

Brown turned and this time smiled with his entire face.

"Honey, you're a awfully terrible liar. Too many details, for one thing. A bunch of other things, too, but I ain't up for making you better at fooling people." He patted her leg. With his free hand he took a pint of liquor from his pocket and turned it up twice. "Do me a favor, you tell Nick I'm already busy enough keeping his butt out of a sling. I'm too old for much more. Now, I'm walking on home. It wouldn't hurt my feelings one bit to see him there at some point before daybreak."

Ashley sat with her mouth hanging open. When Brown went on walking in the direction he'd been going, Nick looked over his shoulder and she gave him a thumbs up. She was mostly grateful she hadn't needed to deal with Fay Mullins. She told herself he might not even have a good idea of what she looked like this far away in the dark. She could be anybody as far as he knew. Until Nick came back to the shelter, she watched smoke rolling from somebody's fireplace across the small hill behind the park. It rolled white and thick and when it reached the stars, the stars disappeared, just faint flickers behind the thinning plumes.

"We're all the way set, now," Nick said.

But Ashley had already found a quiet place inside her head with whoever burned that fire across the hill, inside a warm living room glowing like an angel in a picture-book bible.

21

The bag came from Brown's time overseas. Like a lot of men returning, he held to everything he could. It was a strange thing, he figured, to want to keep things from that place, that time. They'd taken his M-16 like it was nothing more than a backpack only needed for a long walk in the woods. And maybe that's all it was all along. Like the religion his sister and his mother held onto through their lives. The more he thought about that, the more he figured this notion was about right. Religion was just the weapon you carried with you through life, everybody's war, and then it was checked at the gates of Heaven before they sent you on home. But the bag came in handy today, now, this moment.

Brown pulled the bag closer to his side. He had nothing but good memories from his time overseas. *That's the truth nobody knew.* Since coming home he'd been labeled a baby killer and a murderer, and things were already bad enough for him and his family when he went into the military. Coming home and having that much more to carry around had put Brown down so low, he hadn't bothered telling any of them he'd been stationed in Korea and put in charge of a maintenance garage. Ate breakfast every morning in dry clothes, listened to the radio or watched television in the evenings, had plenty to drink, saw women on the occasion it moved him to do so, had plenty of smokes. The war was the only time in his life when life was normal. Everybody looked the same, dressed the same, had the same amount of food and access to vehicles. If you were better than someone else, you had earned that right. You had the stripes to show for it and there was no need to go around bragging about it or putting others down for it. Whatever meanness Brown had was already there, had been beaten into him a long time before he was old enough to sign up or get drafted. But he didn't have combat experience or training that made him any more mean than the average guy who had been through hard times. Most of that myth started with Nick when he was really young, not long after he was able to understand that Brown had been in the Army. Next thing, Nick was telling people his uncle had been a soldier, which wasn't false at all. But after a couple years, Nick built him up, stacking story after story to overtake the harshness of the locals, the mocking, and all the rest. By the time Brown was taking him for their little training sessions in the field, Brown wasn't so sure he hadn't bought into a lot of it himself.

When he got home and the bad treatment started again, instead of explaining, Brown tucked that time in the military down inside himself. It was a place and time he remembered with fondness, a remembered memento for his heart only. He did try to share some of that while he was there, though. He remembered writing notes back home from the tops of mountains on the outskirts of Ascom Depot, Company B. to Mary and their mother. He wanted to explain his new place and how good things were for him. They wrote back asking if he was being shot at or was he shooting at anybody else. Had he killed anybody? Hadn't he even been shot at? He found the letters later on, shoved back into the hutch drawer on the coffee table in the living room. He told Mary in the letters about managing shipments of various items here and there, about the television shows, the chow hall food compared to the field mess he only ever tried for the experience. It was all there, proof enough that his service was entirely different than anything folks in town would have imagined. And he didn't stay quiet about the truth of it to keep up any sort of mean reputation. *Down to brass tacks*, Brown let them think whatever they wanted to think because they were going to torture him either way. *Better to be feared and reviled and mocked than be a laughing joke and mocked.*

A week into his service, Brown knew he wanted to be a military man. He was sure that had they sent him directly to the front lines, he would have felt the same. The sameness, the clear lines drawn among people by fairness and respect, small pleasures. These were things home didn't offer. So he worked hard. He took extra shifts on watch, usually when they were watching from the mountains so he could sit and think and smoke cigarettes and listen to how a place as new to him as Korea sounded in the night. His last night on watch he was deep into the sounds of a powerful rainstorm, how it rushed all around him and filled up the ground until all of it might have been soaked cornbread they walked across the next morning for regular exercise. The day following that last watch and the morning exercise, Brown made the biggest mistake a soldier could make in rain country. He didn't shower after the hike, and the stripes had taken all of them directly from watch to exercise. All of this added up to Brown's wearing rain-soaked socks just long enough in that humid place for him to develop gangrene. Foot rot kept him out of the military, ended it sooner and left him aggravating problems with it in the years following so that reenlisting wasn't much of an option.

Thing was, he had a war on his hands now. Stan Collins was nowhere to be seen. He'd usually come out around this time and fool around with his fall beans. But the house was still in the distance. Then, just when Brown had started thinking of a drink, he saw Stan ease out to the porch. The screen door screeched and then banged shut, a muffled sound from this distance. Brown checked his handgun again, then looked to his mother in Heaven.

Never one to pray, exactly, feeling unworthy to offer words to Heaven, Brown now spoke in a whisper, explaining this was an act needed for her blessed grandbaby in the absence of her lost daughter who cared not a whit or had done a single thing that wasn't just plain selfish. He finished and took a quick stock of the path he would make to the house.

Brown looked one last time at the 9mm held loosely in his hand, offered a pause, mostly out of respect to his mother and partly in respect to what he was about to do, and started on his belly through the dying corn stalks. The forty or so feet to get within a good distance of Stan's front porch wasn't any more distance than he had crawled before, but the stalks were the real problem. What would have taken no more than ten minutes even at his age now and less as a young man instead was nearly an hour of soil up his nose and crows flying low to his location and his elbows aching from dragging himself and keeping his legs from hooking stalks.

He came to the edge of the short distance that had taken him so long to cover and eased into a squatting position. Brown looked back at garden, that field of tired corn and craggy arms of marijuana plants growing sideways through cinder blocks about every five feet or so, and for a flighty moment thought how silly he had been. He should have walked straight to the door and did what was needed without all the show and tactics. But all that poop had kept him alive this long, belly crawling, hidden bunkers in his and Nick's field. The cabin where Tucker waited now and would wait as long as Brown needed him to wait. No, even with or without Heaven's help, the way he conducted business was the only way for someone like him.

Stan hadn't returned to the porch, and both the screen door and front door were now closed. Brown had been in the house twice before, years ago when things were different. He recalled a back door in the kitchen. That's how he'd get in, through the back door, like a coward.

Getting through the lock on the back door took longer than Brown expected. Every click of his knife against metal or knock of his elbow against wood sounded like gunshots in his head. All this paranoia was for nothing, more or less. Stan was as much of a drunk as he was these days. He was likely prone on his bed with a pint of 100 proof watching some random television program and waiting to nod off and be out of this world. Brown understood the notion well enough, that black place where thought was out of your hands and God took over, showing you the worries and burdens in coats of merciful darkness. Stan was in that land, or close.

Brown let go his guard and pushed against the door with the hunting knife wedged hard into the bolt lock. The door popped loose and the scent of dirty dishes wafted out into the fall air. *And something else. A strong scent, pleasant and familiar. Old Spice.* Brown pushed the door open and saw Stan sitting in a kitchen chair pulled out from the table. He sipped from a cup of coffee. His eyes were set and clear. Brown opened his mouth to speak and Stan waved him off.

"I think we've done about enough talking," he said. As casual as could be, he sat his coffee cup in the floor beside him. "Stand on up, Brown."

Realizing just then he was still bent in place from picking the door loose, Brown stood. His bag was two feet to his left, just out of sight, but his 9mm was tucked into the back of his pants. *No guns to speak of near Stan. Enough talking.* That hit Brown's ear about right. He pulled his gun and walked to Stan and sited him in, a smooth spot between his eyes.

But something was off. Brown heard a slow shuffle of boots against hardwood from the living room, muffled grunting, and the sounds of a weak struggle. And then Fay Mullins was standing at the kitchen table. Stan didn't bother to look behind him to the doorway. He stared blankly at the pinpointed barrel of Brown's gun. Fay had Hen by the arm. Brown couldn't see a place on her that wasn't bruised or bleeding–face, forehead, arms, neck. He recognized Fay as the man in the park with Nick and Ashley, but that did nothing but shutter his mind. He focused.

Holding a six-shot pistol to Hen's head, Fay reached into his coat and pulled one baggie after another from his coat pocket and tossed them on the kitchen table. Inside some were pills, others were filled to busting with pot, and in a third was what looked to be cocaine. He paused, switched the pistol to his other hand and fought off a weak struggle from Hen until he could reach into the other pocket. Five more baggies of pills. They took up most of the surface space of Stan and Hen's small kitchen table.

"I don't mind chatting a bit," Fay said. He allowed Hen to drop into a kitchen chair. Stan reached for her across the table, a subtle gesture, and Fay swiped his hand back. "None of that, though, lovebirds."

Hen spat on him, a combination of blood and the deep chest phlegm of a longtime smoker, a red mass that landed in a swatch across Fay's neck. His smile was unsettling, full of yellow, squared hog's teeth. The morning chill was moving off across the mountains in a ghost-fog, burned away by the rising sun, warming the house. Fay pulled off his coat and let it drop to the floor. He was strapped, two handguns hugging his sides. He adjusted them and walked to the sink, speaking to Brown rather than acknowledging Stan.

"She was a tough one, a good old lady. Took me most of the morning to get it out of her where she had her goods stashed away. I found Tuck's in no time. Seems Tuck dipped a fraction into his goods and spent too little time finding a comfy spot to keep 'em away from prying hands." Fay held up his hands and wiggled his fingers. Hen's bloody spittle had dripped from his neck to below the neckline of his shirt. "I thought it'd be the other way round, considering that old lady of Dan Bell's spilled where she got her dope in no time. Didn't have to rough her up much at all. Just as much as I wanted before it, you know, just come to be a bit boring. Seems her and Henry here been doing some fine amount of business. A bonus, as I was only to be compensated for ushering Tuck out of this world. Kid gets his dope and I get paid. But you know I got me some cake *and* pie, a little taste of my own. I love when a plan just flourishes like that. Don't you, Brown Bottle?"

Behind Fay, Stan stared across the table at Hen. She had her head down, either from guilt or pain or both, Brown couldn't tell. Brown felt Fay's fingers clutch his cheeks, turn his face toward him.

Fay Mullins, Heaven have mercy, and here I am on the floor like a fool hiding from a tornado already inside the house. He swallowed and felt the dry click in his throat. Fay was so close in on him, he wondered if he could have heard it, that weak click, the way a wild dog could sense a limp from the sound of off-beat footsteps, a broken stride. His plan to have it out with Stan seemed thought up in another life or some meshed up rant during a drinking blackout.

"Let go my face," Brown said. It came out less forceful as he would have liked, considering Fay still held him firmly along the jawline.

Fay grinned. His eyes were empty as the sky. He released Brown and turned to look at Stan, then swiveled back to examine Brown. He did this a couple of times and then grinned again.

"You boys got your own situation, I see that," he said. "Like always, I'm just on a job. In all the wretched decades I've been here, you hillbillies still confound me with your reasoning. I've come to learn the only good reason for bloodshed is money. But I believe we can figure this out. I have some time, and I do love a good brawl."

Fay pulled loose his gun straps and tossed them in the kitchen sink, and carefully placed his pistol beside the dish drainer. He moved in Brown's direction and Brown stayed perfectly still. When Fay grabbed the bag he'd brought home with him from the desert, he took Fay's arm, dug his fingers deep enough to feel the tendons there shift and move aside for purchase on solid bone.

"Easy, soldier. Just bear with me, huh? A little patience."

Brown sickened at how soft and easy Fay's voice was in the middle of this ruin. He wondered why Stan and Hen only sat there like pine knots and didn't offer once to take this man from behind when they had every chance in the God-given world.

22

It was a fight Fay wanted, more than the money, even. More than the drug haul. He wanted blood. It wasn't an idea, an urge, Brown was unfamiliar with by a long shot. The kitchen went quiet. Fay had Stan and Hen wrapped up at the table like prisoners of war, broken and now spending time imagining how they might die, hoping it was at least fast.

Brown, let loose from his place on the floor, now stood in front of Fay. It was then he noticed he was a good three inches taller than this terror of a man, this bane on the county, this man who deemed himself a killer.

"Take a gun from the sink," Fay said.

Stan and Hen motioned with quick nods. *Yes, yes, yes,* they said without a word.

"I think I'll be fine, you butthole."

"Butthole! Butt. Hole!" Fay pulled back his lips to show those yellowed hog chompers again. Laughing he turned back to Stan and jabbed a thumb in Brown's direction. "Butthole," he said again, and laughed until his smoker's cough cut him off. When Fay turned, quick as a flash Brown pulled loose a length of steel cable wire from his belt loops and quick as a flame he had the wire around Fay's neck. Brown pulled up and away and listened for the crack of bone, felt for the lack of movement, but there was none. Fay only slumped to the floor, one arm reaching for the sink.

The back door came open, loudly. Ashley stood shaking with a rifle held on Fay, with Nick right behind her. Brown let loose his steel wire and allowed Fay to stand. Fay smiled and started to say something, but Ashley interrupted him by firing off two shots, one sending a bullet into his upper right thigh and another missing entirely and shedding a cabinet above the kitchen sink. Fay slumped to the floor, one hand holding himself from falling out completely on the floor, the other grasping for this young girl still holding a gun on him.

"Get out," Ashley said. She sounded older, angrier.

Fay took one last lunge toward her. Brown gave an inverted kick to the killer's kneecap. The snap of bone giving was audible and sweet. Ashley handed the rifle to Brown and he passed it along to Nick.

"Ain't gonna need that to get this piece of crap out of here," Brown said. He grabbed Fay by the hair of the head and pulled him into the back yard. There he beat him with his hands and his boots until Fay stopped moving. When Fay was still, Brown positioned the man's face and drew back his fist. Fay's nose exploded, and instant swelling developing around his deadened eyes.

Brown leaned in close to Fay's wrecked face and body. "I ain't calling the cops. I'm gonna let you crawl right on out of here on that yeller belly of yours. Let you get back some strength, cause we're gonna finish this right. I'm gonna take you out of this world. Get good and healthy before you come see me again. I don't want you making excuses when I send you to Hell."

Fay lay motionless.

"Get moving," Brown said. "Grab hold of some grass, drag your dirty rotten self out of our sight."

Fay did just that, crawling along through the yard, making not a single sound, hardly breathing.

23

Dan woke before daylight. The Alpine Inn needed new bulbs. He turned on every light in the room and still felt sleepy. He stopped into the bathroom and flicked the switch. *Good lights in the bathroom.* He stood at the mirror and rubbed his eyes. If he still drank coffee he'd brew a cup with the packets lining the sink outside the bathroom. No rest after about midnight, when he had thought Lana would call. This wasn't his first night at the Alpine in the last couple months. By now she knew the routine, and he didn't change it up. More and more Dan could see his staying at the inn becoming a permanent thing. Only the idea of Ashley left to handle things on her own kept him coming back home. But that's not where he was heading this morning. He needed a solid trail to follow and that meant finding out where Brown was spending his time off the grid.

There were no offices at the sheriff's department, save for the sheriff's, a former coal truck driver turned deputy once the coal boom during the seventies dried up. Sheriff Henry Ferrari. He told Dan several times, in both public and private conversations, that it was a thousand wonders a grandson of immigrants ever got a political seat in Port County, adding it must have been his size that helped. Ferrari was more than six and a half feet tall and weighed in at about three-hundred twenty pounds. Most of it still muscle, though he was just about ten years from retirement age. So, he had the only office, and no one asked for their own.

The morning after finding Ashley at home with Lana, Dan sat outside Ferrari's office watching his dispatcher wife print out flyers for that year's Shop-With-A-Cop event.

"He busy today?" Dan asked. Kelly Ferrari was easily fifteen years the sheriff's junior. *Slim, blonde, not smart, loyal—little to nothing about her that comes as a surprise.*

"Always busy," Kelly said without looking up from the copier. "What you needing?"

"Just a few questions on something I know about that's brewing."

"Brewing?"

"Not brewing like moonshine," he said. "Just something that might get started up here soon. Something I wanted to give him a heads up about."

"I knew you weren't talking about moonshine, Dan. Good lord." She shook her head and walked off with a chop in her step.

"She thought I was talking about moonshine," Dan said to the empty office just before Ferrari swung open his door and waved him in.

"What're we doing?" Ferrari asked. He always acted rushed, and those were always his first three words to anyone who came to see him.

Dan explained the situation with Stan Collins and Wade "Brown Bottle" Taylor, Nick Taylor, the near overdose, Tuck Collins. Ferrari's eyes lit up when he mentioned Tuck.

Ferrari placed his hands palm down on his desk and leaned in. Brown could see the comb marks in his hair, hair so black it's like some kind of dark hole in the top of his head. "That's the gamey little bastard we've been sitting on since our last drug roundup, right?"

"Yessir."

Of the fifteen people arrested in the last roundup in July, eight of them agreed to point in the right direction, tell the department where they made their regular buys. All eight pointed to Tuck and received probated sentences. Of those eight, three agreed to be wired and take part in controlled buys. So far nothing. Not one good buy, and the papers were starting to write stories about how eight out of fifteen alleged drug dealers arrested in July had served not a single day of jail time. That's how it read in the paper, *not a single day*, and *alleged drug dealers*. Couldn't go in and tell the paper it was because they snitched and agreed to cooperate. Couldn't further explain that none of them were drug dealers, clear up that they were drug buyers. The whole thing made for bad press and Ferrari had only the current year remaining before it was time to start campaigning again.

"Okay, okay," Ferrari said. "What're we doing?"

Dan relaxed. He asked for a cup of coffee and if there were any aspirin around. Ferrari opened his top drawer and tossed over a bottle of Tylenol, motioned to the coffee pot. Dan stepped quickly, poured himself a cup and swallowed the pill with the first sip. He sat down and detailed his general idea. He told Ferrari he'd been thinking about this for the last few days. There was a guy in for a probation violation, Doug Hall, who was a good friend of Brown's. If he could help them locate Brown, it might mean the difference between handling a minor dispute and something much worse. Everybody knew that drinking didn't dull Brown's propensity for violence. *Made it worse, if anything.*

"You think they'd be some killing come out of this?" Ferrari asked. Dan couldn't tell if he could hear excitement or fear in the sheriff's voice, or both.

"Maybe so," he said. "But if I can get to Brown first, we avoid that. And, let's just be honest here." Dan stopped, he was about to step out onto some rotted wood. "Let's be honest, Tuck Collins ain't much use to you dead. Not politically, I mean."

Ferrari's far off expression didn't change. He leaned back into his chair and it popped beneath his weight.

"And we got this Hall guy in lockup right now, huh?" It wasn't a question. He laced his hands behind his head. "Okay, yep, let's do that. That's what we're doing."

And before Dan knew it, he stood outside the office again, watching the copier spit out papers. He took a piece of peppermint candy from the counter and headed to the jail.

In the booking area of the detention center was an office—bare, a metal table and two chairs, but it was an office and that meant privacy, which Dan would need while talking to Doug Hall.

Hall had been arrested on a minor violation of the terms of his probation four days ago. Crossing state lines. But it was still a minor violation in Port County. A lot of people drove across the line to Virginia on Sunday to buy alcohol. The only difference is that Hall had been caught doing it. Dan had done the same thing more times than he could remember while in high school. At least Hall was of age. Still, Hall was a regular at the jail. And he was smart in the way a prisoner needed to be smart.

He looked smart coming around the corner, staring with a grin into the glassed off room where inmates met with their legal representatives. He grinned like he knew they weren't lawyers, like he'd already learned a long time ago they were court appointed attorneys who could not possibly give two shits less about anyone in that jail. But he was smart in here, not so much on the outside. It was a thousand wonders Doug Hall wasn't already serving long time in the federal pen up at Inez.

"Howdy, Dan," Doug said before sitting down at the table.

Dan didn't waste any time. "I need to know where I can find Brown Bottle, Doug. I might can help you with these last charges if you help us."

Doug scratched his nose and when he did his handcuffs rattled like bracelets. He exaggerated the sound by shaking his hands more than needed, scratching his nose for longer than necessary.

"Take them off," Dan told the guard, who was already walking away. He looked put out, having to turn back and unlock the cuffs. Dan didn't recognize him and figured he was probably about two weeks on the job.

"It's a time thing, Doug," he continued. "I believe he's about to get into some real heavy lifting, and it's likely to not end good for him if I can't catch up with it."

Dan wasn't sure if Doug was able to see he was sincere, but he shifted in his seat and leaned in closer. His eyebrows drew down, his mouth lost that playful, knowing grin.

"It have to do with Nick?" Doug asked.

"I think so, yeah. How'd you know that?" Dan immediately felt both embarrassed and hopeful. Doug was about Brown's only friend. It made sense that he would know what was going on with him lately. It was exactly the reason he had come to visit him. *Information. If he knows the dilemma with Nick, he might surely know where to find Brown.*

"I'm going to save you a lot of time here, Dan," Doug said. "Get this probation shit wiped out and I'll tell you exactly where he's at, no problem. I'll tell you right now, so long as you can get Judge Deskins on that phone over there and get me walking with you out those doors."

"Okay, that's fine. Where can I get to Brown?"

The grin reappeared. "Not till you do just what I said."

"I don't really have time for this, Doug. There's no way I can move those wheels that fast, but I'll start them rolling a little." He stopped and motioned for Molly Newsome, the guard who had been working the longest, knew the ropes and just how far they all had to stretch them.

Molly stepped over and Dan, while looking at Doug, asked her to get Judge Deskins on the phone as fast as she could. Told her to get him over there so he could talk to him on the line as soon as she could. She nodded and when she walked back to the counter, she picked up a phone and within a second or two was talking. A few seconds later, she waved him over.

"It's Giovanni's," Molly said in a low whisper when Dan leaned down to her. "We're eating there for lunch today. Right here on this paper is what everybody wants. Just sit right down here and order for us. Thanks, Danny."

Dan sat down and ordered a pizza bread, two loaded cheeseburgers, cheese sticks, and three orders of large fries. It took about three minutes, and Doug watched every move he made. Once, right before the young girl on the other end asked if it would be a pick up or a delivery, Dan gave Doug a thumbs up. Was it too much? He watched Doug for signs of distrust and saw none. He needed to remember to bring something nice for Molly next time he was in.

Doug shook his head like a disapproving parent when Dan sat back down in front of him. "That ain't going to do, officer," he said.

"Well, it's going to have to do," Dan answered. He tried to seem as confident as possible. Doug's eyes were reptilian in their examination of him. "Deskins is game for reviewing and considering."

"Bullshit."

"What do you want me to tell you, Doug? The man's going to review and consider. It's what you've got. It's more than you had fifteen minutes ago."

Doug looked off, a dramatic sweep of hair and chin. He leaned in again and Dan thought to himself that a nice box of cinnamon candy might do perfectly for Molly.

"Jesus Christ," Doug said, "I can't believe you ain't found it with all the pointless pot stash hunts you guys go on all summer long. Wade's got a cabin. Damn, he's had it since we were kids, for crissakes. Go up John Attic Ridge starting at White Mountain just above the old Damron place and just hang right along the auger road. That's where he's going to be, if he ain't crazy as a coon and hiding in him and Nick's little foxhole out there by their apartment. If he's down in there, then he's too far gone for any of you to bring back. Pack a gun."

Dan knew the auger road Doug mentioned. And it was unbelievable they had hadn't come across it in all these years, but they hadn't. Brown probably camouflaged it during summer.

"Thanks, Doug, really. I'm just trying to keep some peace. Can't hold that against a guy, surely."

"I can if you're lying to me about the judge," he said. "And I think you are, Dan."

"Would Molly do you wrong?"

"Yes, Molly would do me wrong. All of you would."

24

The fallout at Stan and Hen's was over by then. They all scattered once Fay crawled away. It was mostly a tangled mess, and it wasn't nearly finished, but it was settled enough. Before leaving, there had been a surreal conversation between them during which all agreed to leave authorities out. Stan tended to Hen while Hen tried to tend to the upturned house. Nick and Ashley, speaking to no one, left first, Nick looking at Brown as they walked out the door. It had been the same look he gave Brown when he was younger, like he wanted to hold onto him with his eyes. What was unsaid is that no one had the feeling that anything had been settled. It was more like leaving to get rest on the second day of a three-day funeral. It was Stan who convinced the rest to keep the law out of it for now. "Too much to explain," he had said. And so they left.

Wherever the rest landed, Brown had his own unfinished issue at the cabin. He knew Tuck might already be dead, but he couldn't get himself to make it through the hills to the cabin any faster than a stroll. It was part adrenaline and a quiet satisfaction from deep inside. But if he were to tell the truth, the liquor had a lot to do with it. After the quick discussion at Stan and Hen's, there was some hanging around, a little more talk about whether or not someone should at least get hold of Dan. But Brown didn't join in. He had slipped outside, saying he needed air. He hadn't needed air. He had needed a drink, and went directly to take care of that first.

About halfway along the ridgeline heading to the cabin, Brown stopped and took another pull from the bottle. It hit his throat hard and he had a fast gag reflex before it settled in his stomach. After he had left Stan and Hen's, he caught a ride with Seth Tackett. Seth dropped him at Food City and, instead of walking the next mile to Crow Hill Spirits and Wine, he bought two fifths in their drinks section. High end stuff and, since he hadn't been drinking much lately, he was having a harder time keeping it down than he would have imagined. The first fifth went slowly. He had sat in the field and drank it with a six pack of Coke. He fell asleep examining his skinned knuckles, swelled from impact against Fay's cheekbones. When he woke, he started immediately for the cabin.

He was going to let Tuck go, no question about that. It was due time to let go of all this Nick and drugs business. Not one good thing had come out of his trying. If anything it had gotten worse, ending with Fay. Ending for him and Nick, at least. The Collins had their own problems, and the Bells, too. Best thing he could do was turn Tuck loose, find Nick, and work on a plan for getting him to Ohio. Ohio wasn't a lot better than Kentucky, but it was one or two steps in a different direction, even if it wasn't exactly the right direction. After that, it was more or less drinking and the madness that came from it.

He had filled the whiskey washtub with water from a natural spring and left it close enough for Tuck to drink, but if he was being honest before God, before now he had sort of forgotten about Tuck entirely. *Most anybody would've,* Brown thought, but it still didn't sit well with him that he could forget about a human being that easily, even a human being as smudged as Tuck Collins. He snapped dead branches as he made his way closer to the where the cabin was perched on the ridge. He'd rather have Tuck know he was coming and be ready with whatever kind of crazy talk he needed to get out of his system than to surprise him. If he had a mobile phone he would have called Nick before he started up this way, had Nick call Ashley. There were a lot of moving parts to all of this, and if he could get them all in one place maybe he had a better chance of making it right, getting Nick as far away from him and the world of this hard place.

This thought, a life without Nick at its center, hit him with gale-force in the trembling of his guts. He took another long pull of liquor, Red Stag, a sweeter drink than he was used to but good for now, strong and warm. *Nick's gonna have to make it on his own now. I done all I can and the rest's up to him.* It was an idea living only in his head for now. His heart didn't believe any of it possible.

When he could make out the cabin, he stopped and checked his boot laces. Too many times he had needed to high tail it out of the woods and been caught by stray boot laces. He didn't figure he'd need to be doing much running from this situation, but, like all the rest of it, who could know? Still squatting beside a leaning mimosa tree, he finished off the Red Stag, gagged almost enough to send it back up, and regained his composure. Shaking the bitterness off, he closed the rest of the distance to where Tuck most likely sat fuming.

As soon as Brown opened the door to the cabin, he could smell that familiar stench. Someone's bowels had moved, and recently. You caught that smell all the time in the military, especially in battle. Tuck was slumped in the corner. The washtub had been turned over and the spilled water had soaked Tuck's pants. Brown could see he had soiled himself. A sorry sight, and one that could have been avoided. Seeing Tuck like that and knowing it was his fault made Brown feel low, even with a good drunk on.

"Tuck," Brown said calmly.

No movement, and some darkness like a thick, deep shadow spreading out from his left side.

"Tuck!" Brown moved across the cabin, pressing his nose into the bend of his elbow and squinting to get a better look. "Get up there, Tucker!"

Still nothing. Brown nudged the top of Tuck's head, hoping to stir him awake, but his head lopped to the side and, when it did, gravity worked in such a way that his entire head from the collarbone up nearly split off from his body. Fresh blood seeped up to the opened gash that ran from just above his shoulder to his left ear. Brown had only a few seconds to recognize what looked like a shaft of white plumbing pipe as Tuck's windpipe cropped up from the meat of his neck muscles before the door slammed behind him.

The first thing Brown noticed about Fay was how calm he was in the doorway. He was holding a pistol like an afterthought. There was blood on his hands and when Brown turned, Fay ran his fingers through his graying hair leaving streaks of it throughout. The sight of it blurred in Brown's vision and he had a memory of a bird he once shot dying on the ground, its blood oil-slicked across its feathers in the exact same way.

"I'm tired, Brown Bottle. Pitifully tired," Fay said. "And more than a little bruised, mostly on the inside, you know, my pride, after that decent little beatdown you gave me. It was all I could do to make that cut there." He pointed to Tuck's lopped sideways head. "And I just flat out could not get the head clean off. Just gave out. Guess I'm getting older. No use denying it anymore."

Fay smiled and looked at the floor, shook his head as if contemplating how bad a winter it had been or how much more he needed to do to fix his car engine, some small thing thought of in passing.

"I can smell the liquor from here, friend," Fay said. "That don't bode well for you, I imagine. It'll be a speck harder to get the best of me this time." Then he looked at the pistol, as if seeing it for the first time. "Well, and this don't hurt."

Brown shuffled his left foot, testing how tuned in Fay was, and when he didn't react, he took the opportunity to edge a full step closer to where Fay stood in the doorway. It could be messy this way, but Brown didn't see a lot of other options.

"What happened to dumping the firearms and being men?" Brown asked, shuffling a little closer when he saw Fay didn't look directly at him when he spoke. He wanted to cover his nose again from the stench, and the Red Stag was threatening to come up from deep in his belly. He tried to forget about Tuck behind him all nearly cut in half. "I'm tired, too. Let's just call it a day and walk away, what's say? I mean, what in the world is in it for you at this point? I don't even know what you're deal is in the first place. You that bad hooked on drugs, or just that bad hooked on killing folks?"

Fay thought being drunk was a strike against Brown, but Brown knew different. He was sharper drunk, more mean, and more deliberate with his meanness. The only thing discouraging to him now was that this mess was in no way going to get sorted out soon. *Not today, not next week, not next month.* The thing was, Stan Collins was a man you didn't want as an enemy, just like himself. And Dan Bell was a cop with a wife who had been assaulted in who knows how many ways. Now Fay had more enemies than anyone could handle, and at least one who would drop him in an open hole in the ground without thinking twice, if it came to that.

Then Fay said something that made all the difference.

"I don't think I'm much interested in all this anymore," he said. "I agree, Brown Bottle. Let's just walk away. Think you can do that? Think you can do that even if your nephew is in the same shape as that waif back there?"

Brown stopped his idle shuffling advance. "What'd you say?"

"You heard me," Fay said. "Nick and that little girl of his, that Bell girl. What if they're in no better shape than old Stan's brother back there? Still want to walk away?"

The line that broke from time to time in Brown broke again. He dropped his arms to his side and walked the three or four steps over to Fay, doing so suddenly Fay was unable to make any sort of move to thwart it. Fay was raising the pistol, but Brown was already on him. Instead of grabbing the gun from Fay's hand, which he could have done without much trouble, Brown took the gun and lifted it to his forehead. Fay's eyes were wide and Brown noticed then that he did look tired, crazy and tired of being crazy. He looked like the old man he really was and always had been at that moment.

"Come to think of it, I'm not sure I much feel like walking just now," Brown said. "Go on ahead and pop that trigger. Go on!"

A fleeting interest went over Fay's face and Brown could see he was trying to read if he was bluffing.

"I don't feel like doing that, Brown Bottle. Your nephew's fine and that little hotshot girl of his is somewhere patting herself on the back for putting a bullet through me, I'm sure. She's about as crazy as I am." Fay looked over Brown's face a full ten seconds and lowered the pistol. "Or crazy as you. Maybe."

Brown steadied himself, tried to take air through his mouth instead of his nose and failed. A series of throaty coughs issued from him, forced the air out and he had to suck in a large amount to get his wind back. He pulled his shoulders back and focused to keep from retching. The familiar scent threatened to send him back to his teen years turning twenty in a rice field while it rained. He was drifting out to that place, and drifting could get him just as dead and rotting as Tuck. He steadied himself and tried to right his mind toward Fay.

25

Like a camera dropping, there was the green-brown wash of the tilted earth, the rounded rock bones of the mountain, the patchwork of sky through the treetops, and there was a heaviness in Brown's stomach, a dread. Then again the scent of a rotting body. The drifting was easing up, lasting only a few seconds, and Brown came out of it talking.

"I don't take pleasure in it, but killing a man ain't nothing to me," he heard himself saying. "They've all thought I killed children around here, so what's one old man gonna matter? I ain't got a shred of reputation to uphold. No reason at all to do anything other than end you."

Brown stopped talking. His vision blurred, but he could make out Fay Mullins—his shape, his stance, that cock-sure way he had of holding himself.

"What in the hellfire you talking about, killing children? Jesus H. Christ."

Fay's voice, that creeping sound he made when he strung words together, was muffled at best. But with the blurry outline and that creeping sound, Brown steadied himself enough to understand.

"Enough talking," Brown said. It was hardly more than a polite and restrained cough coming from him. He tried to give his breath, his speech, as much force as he could.

When nothing, no station as it were, changed to his liking, Brown let it rip. Swinging away, he connected.

His right hook could have landed across Fay's jaw, it could have landed in his stomach, it could have landed against the easy bark of a young tree. But it landed, and the blur left his field of vision. When he heard a grunt coming from somewhere below him, Brown figured he'd landed it well enough.

Follow the grunting sounds Brown found Fay twisted on the ground outside the cabin, his hand cradling an already swollen jawline. When Fay saw Brown leaning over to take hold of him, the grunts became hacked up words full of fluid and rasp. Brown bent closer to pull him upright and Fay lunged and fell further down the hill, stopping only when he connected with another tree.

With everything going on, Brown had turned off his ears from the sounds of the woods. Had he been able to hear the footsteps coming, chances are he could have said he had discovered Fay there against the tree. As it turned out, Dan Bell saw enough when he circled around the cabin from the other side of the auger road with two more deputies behind him, pistols in hand.

"Stop! Get your damn hands in the air, Brown! Get your hands up! Now!"

Brown raised his hands and turned around. Fay started laughing, easy and soft at first and then a hard belly laugh that spiraled up through the treetops and around the valley like a manic ghost of a thing. Dan was drawn down on Brown and so were the two deputies.

"Hiya, Dan," Brown said calmly, though slurred. "Reckon you'll need those other two boys to shoot after you've had your turn?" Brown didn't ask how Dan found them here, but a thought did occur to him, even while Fay still laughed and laughed. "Where's Nick?"

None of the three answered, but Dan lowered his pistol and stepped toward Brown. He looked tired and ragged, as much as the rest of them had become over the past few weeks. Gray pillows hung beneath his eyes from which no light shown, only a flat and dull plate of brown and streaked-red whites. *Likely his daughter's already being held on attempt charges. Maybe Nick's with her*, Brown thought.

"You got Nick and your girl somewhere locked up, Dan? I know that's got to be hard and I'm just asking how Nick is, same as you'd be asking how your girl is."

"My girl and your nephew are locked up," Dan said. "Now, do you figure I'd have any problem locking you up along with Mr. Mullins here?"

Brown squatted, his knees pushed up just enough for him to wrap his arms around them. It was his way of sitting when no chair was available, learned from Joe Halbert, a fellow soldier. Brown liked to call it the Halbert Squat to remember Joe.

When Dan stepped closer and the deputies with him lowered their guns, Brown pushed his hand into his boot. He felt for his knife but when he had his fingers around the handle, it slipped behind his heel and out of reach. When Dan and his deputies joined them at the tree where Fay still lay, quiet now, broken and staring away from the sudden company of police officers, Brown stood, held his hands in the air and walked to Dan. He turned and positioned his hands behind his back. He listened for the deputy to pull the cuffs from his belt and shifted to the left. In this single motion, he took the deputy's gun and shot Fay dead. He turned to the deputies and Dan. He no longer cared where he pointed the gun. The hammer was falling before his eyes settled anywhere.

Dan pulled his eyes away from Fay bleeding out from the neck, slumped against the trees and came to his senses enough to take a sideways dive onto his elbow when Brown turned toward them. From the ground, Dan could almost see the round from the gun Brown fired moving slow through the air, making its personal little tunnel across the space and headed toward Ronnie Dean Sanders, the younger of the two deputies. Ronnie Dean took one in the left shoulder. The hole appeared as a small, red dot in his uniform top. No trickle of blood, no flailing backwards. The youngest deputy might have not been touched by anything at all, let alone having just took a bullet through the shoulder blade. Dan heard a second shot and watched the older of the two deputies slump to his knees. The boy had taken a shot to the kneecap. The bullet exited at the bend in the back of his knee, spraying bone as it went.

For Dan it was a photoflash inside half a moment, and before he could turn to see Brown standing above the three men he had just shot, there were only trees and ground, the scent of the fired gun and of coppery blood and the odd hint of death excrement coming from a still Fay Mullins. There stood no Brown where there had been before, but he could hear branches snapping several yards to the west, downhill. All Dan could think to do was follow, stepping over bodies still bleeding warm as he went.

26

Dan's somewhere close behind, Brown thought. He knew that much. No matter how much he would prefer to stay behind and tend to the others, Dan would follow him. Dan might have grown up with most everything handed to him but when he fell, he grew stronger at the breaks. Not that anyone really thought of Dan as a man with strong character, but those were the dumb ones. Brown knew Dan had something to prove. He just needed the right someone to prove it by. *If I could only tell Dan I'm runnin' to keep from killin' him, that might help. But, that's no option now.* Brown was Dan's someone. They were tied together the same as he and Stan were at this point. All of them tangled up together with something bound to break.

To his mind, Brown himself had nothing to prove. His goals had been the same since the day Mary gave birth to Nick. Nothing complicated about his nature after Nick came along. When he pondered on whether or not Nick needed it anymore or cared for it at all, Brown pushed that out of his mind. Pushing things out of his mind was a trick Brown had down to a science. A place like his cabin, a place to go make that happen, was always a help. Now that was gone, too. He'd never feel the same on this mountain again. Brown could already accept this, felt it as he passed along old sections of the hillside where he used to stop and take in a long appreciation of a spiral row of honeysuckles or watch squirrels climb spruce trees to the top and back again. *It's all gonna be like this now*, Brown thought. *A collection of moments changed from the inside out.*

Running downhill was always more like falling, and Brown fell fast, sliding his body left and right to avoid trees. He made a racket cruising downhill that way, so he let his weight slap against a thick cedar and was quiet. The push of grounded leaves skittering across the slope of the hillside settled, and then only the sound of his heart beating in his ears kept Brown from getting a good read on where Dan was behind him. When the thumping in his ears let up, he could barely hear Dan working his way down to him, not falling like he was doing, but moving steadily from one to tree to the next, finding his footing, being careful. It was a foolish thing to do, and Brown figured a man who hadn't been in the hills much would probably ease his way down like that, and that was fine with him. *Take your time*, Brown thought, and spun off the cedar and started falling again.

As he fell, Brown checked the clip in the deputy's gun. He had several left, enough to make him difficult to arrest, in any case. He continued to skip down the hillside and this allowed him to focus on catching onto the trees and not going head-first over a ridge cliff. This Brown focused on, not that he had just gunned down three men. Those deputies just couldn't sit still. At least he only winged them and the only death on his conscious was Fay Mullins. That Brown could live with, push come to shove.

A cracking loose of soft wood came from behind him. Brown remembered passing a wet-rotted birch tree about fifteen long, jumping strides back. *It's Dan.* He was closer than Brown guessed. Positioning his heels downward so the toes of his boots pointed up, he shifted his shoulders and turned in a clunky ballet move. When facing up the hill, he fired two shots one after another. Before taking stock on whether he landed a shot, Brown turned again and started his falling run. By his count, he should have a dozen or so rounds left in the magazine. Probably a dozen with one in the chamber. Without turning he swung his arm back and fired one more shot and grabbed the next tree and kept falling. No time to see if it brought any result.

The walls of his stomach seized violently, and with the taste of vomit still in his throat and mouth, and with an armed man chasing him, Brown felt the deep need for a drink. Just as this thought began to overpower him, he saw a clearing, a flatness of ridgeline. Probably an old auger road when they fixed the gas lines in this area. *Dan'll stop here— no way he won't, winded and runnin' out of adrenaline.*

When he stopped on the auger road the titled world of the hillside righted and Brown became lightheaded from the switch. He remembered his mother saying people from Kentucky walked leaning on flat ground from gardening on a slope for so long.

Dan could see Brown, a tiny moving blight of darkness down the hillside. After radioing in that Evan and Benson were down, he had tried to reposition his walkie and dropped it somewhere in the leaves and mud behind him. At least he got word to the sheriff's office. They were fifteen minutes out and then another twenty getting anywhere near where he was chasing Brown. His was a one-man show in the meantime.

Nick and Ashley were, in fact, locked up. Dan had arrested them in the early morning hours on Yellow Flats. For now they were being held for questioning, but that wouldn't last long. He needed accounts from Hen and Stan and, well, Brown, too, he figured.

He thought about how all that seemed terribly complicated when he was making his way tracking Brown up to the cabin, and how it seemed so irrelevant now while chasing Brown to arrest him on charges of murder and the attempted murder of two police officers. Picturing again the deputies slumping to the ground, he felt immense guilt cradle him to a choking point. And now he was running off a hillside straight into what was going to most likely be a shootout that could not end well.

Two shots came from his not too far left, down the hill, and, about ten feet in that direction, a bullet splintered a small cedar, the pulped wood spraying out from it like rushing blood.

Dan stopped and crouched against a nestle of small cliff rocks, the kind that occasionally seemed to poke out from the hill but had really been there all along and were only now visible because of two-hundred and fifty thousand years of growth and then slow weathering. Dan wished he could somehow crawl beneath of the skin of the hill where the rocks had once been, hide himself the way the bones of the hill did when it was a more proud mountain. But the weather had gotten to him too, and here he was exposed with Brown shooting at him and more hell still to come.

Rising from his spot beside the small set of cliff rocks, Dan thought for a moment about firing a warning shot back, but realized he wasn't at all clear on where Brown was from his line of sight. He might have been lucky with the shot, or unlucky, and hit Brown dead center for all he knew.

Then a terrible beautiful thought occurred to him. If he found Brown, shot and killed him, it would be justifiable and finish this mess. It was as true as true could be. Because if he didn't, and brought Brown in alive, there was Stan and Hen to deal with, especially Stan. With all that had happened, Stan would be crazy for revenge. There had already been trouble between the two of them with just the thought of Brown and Tuck having it out over the drugs. Now Stan would be out for blood, and more blood was not what the situation needed. Except maybe if he shot Brown himself. Just that much blood, and so it would keep anything from growing into a full out no-end-sight war. Stan had a lot of other family in the county—cousins, uncles, nephews—enough to keep this going for several years, a decade maybe. Doing this would end it now, this minute.

27

It was difficult to get a high spot view of the auger road. Brown would have preferred a flat lay, a rifle, a scope, a marker. This dugout patch on the hillside would have to do. It placed him about a hundred feet or so from where Dan should show up on the auger road.

He dug his body deeper into the ground, trying to get all the branches that were going to snap to snap so if he had to reposition with Dan in his line of sight there would be less sound.

He straightened, thinking *Dan must've been lagging further behind than I thought.* Seconds passed and more seconds, and then he heard the sounds of chase coming down from the hill, a cracking of tree branches and shuffling of leaves. It all sounded like Dan was still alone.

Then he saw him, ten feet from the auger road. He was out of breath but still pushing, and Brown at once felt something deep and strong in his gut for Dan Bell, the way he was pushing forward and all of it part of his job, a job he was doing with everything in him. At just about the spot Brown hoped Dan would stand for him to get the best shot, Dan squatted low and touched the ground. He scanned the area with his eyes, his chest still heaving, arms hanging like strung tobacco.

There was a moment when Brown was sure Dan saw him. Their eyes met and Dan kept his gaze trained on him in a focused way that prompted Brown to hold his breath. So intense was Dan's gaze, it seemed Brown could almost count the color specks shooting out from his pupils, all his faculties sharpened with the pistol stretched as far out from his shoulder as possible to get a rifle feel for the shot. When Dan looked away, hearing something move through the tangle to his left, Brown leveled his eye down toward the end of the barrel and squeezed off a shot. It landed near enough to where he intended and opened a nickel-sized hole in Dan's right shoulder.

Now that he had actually shot people, Brown thought of how the movies got the whole deal wrong. A man didn't go flying backwards when a bullet hit him. He just did nothing different. The bullet went through him or lodged in him the way wind would blow through a knothole, clean and fast and leaving the rest standing. That's how it was when Dan took that shot, not so much as rocking an inch one way or the other from his squatted position. Aware enough of the fact he was shot, Dan only stood up and looked to the spot in front of him where he had dropped his gun.

"Now listen, Brown!" Dan called out while holding to his shoulder. There was a fair amount of blood coming already. Brown could see it pushing through his fingers. "Listen here, it don't have to go like this!"

And then Brown heard him mutter "Shit" under his breath and then "Son of a bitch." Brown still had the pistol barrel squared on him. It wasn't like in the movies at all. Dan had stood up and was wandering around on the auger road, looking around with his eyes stretched so big in a scared way that brought that feeling to Brown's gut again, that feeling of brotherhood. *Dan's my brother, the way he's standin' in the middle of the woods doin' his job. Hell, his kin was jailed just same as mine and he ain't shot and killed people and gone crazy. Dan ain't facin' life in prison.*

His shot landed well enough that Dan's good shooting arm was useless. Brown figured he couldn't do much with the left, hadn't practiced with it for this kind of situation. He eased the tension out of his trigger finger and with a grunt he didn't try to hide, he righted himself. He was going in. They'd have to hold him at the county jail awhile before eventually sending him out to LaGrange. Nick would be there and he could apologize to him, apologize for sending everything sideways like this when all he was trying to do was protect him.

As if yelling mercy, he called out for Dan.

Son of a bitch, Dan thought, and tried to imagine a means by which to wrap his shoulder. *Son of a horrid bitch.* Without much luck, he tried to wiggle his fingers and then he heard someone let out a loud sound from the woods. It came from his left, back up the hill, and not very far off.

"Dan Bell!"

Dan's whole body seized, muscles grabbing bone, anticipating another hot bullet before realizing it was a Brown's voice booming out at him.

"Dan! I'm coming in. Don't shoot!"

A pistol came boomeranging out from a treeline to Dan's left. It landed and stuck in the soft ground of the auger road, the butt sticking skyward like a blackened mushroom. Dan made his way across to it and pulled it loose from the ground. At the edge of his field of vision he saw Brown moving down from the hillside. When he turned, he turned with his weapon aimed.

"You've buried yourself. Buried yourself!" Dan said when Brown was in full view. He looked like he hadn't slept in two weeks.

Brown kept making his way down the hill and was almost on the old auger road when Dan stopped him, held up his hand like a traffic cop. "About right there'll do. That's good. Now just ease on down here a couple more feet."

The way Brown moved, easy and gentle with his hands at his sides, his long fingers flexing out and then rolling back up and into his palms, uneased Dan. It reminded him of how animals at the zoo—the big, dangerous animals like a lion or a gorilla—held themselves when people watched them, like they were priming their bodies, working their blood up to a rush.

"Right there'll be just fine," Dan said.

"Ain't armed, Dan," Brown said. He raised his arms and kept them there.

Dan steadied the gun, blocking out Brown's voice, trying not to look directly in his eyes.

There wasn't much honor in it, but this was best. One man killed, if an otherwise decent man, considering what had just happened, was the price to pay for a decade or more of fighting and probably killing. So he fired and Brown bent double, toppling head first onto the flatness of the road. He still looked like a readying animal then, but also nothing more than a tired man who had exhausted himself clawing at things in the dark.

Dan could hear him mumbling, a throaty string of phrases, a series of whisper whines. He had been hoping for a chest shot, but by the way Brown struggled with his hands mashed into his stomach it was more than likely a gut shot. Easing his weapon back into its holster he took careful steps toward Brown until he was standing over him, casting a shadow across the fetal-bent man. Standing there until it was over, he didn't realize how loud Brown's dying was until the last breath was out and gone and the woods returned to the vacuum of quietness found only in places so ancient and hidden away.

EPILOGUE

Nick positioned everything neatly in front of him. Having done so for the third time, he placed his hands behind his head and lay back, closing his eyes. He imagined clouds and the blueness of the sky beyond them. He needed only to open his eyes to see the sky and the clouds from where he lay at the west end of the field. It was humid, the air around him so thick it was like being under water. He thought up a little wind blowing in from a valley somewhere, tried to feel it moving in his hair and across his face. He pictured a day years ago when he first learned to execute a serious leg sweep, pictured how big Uncle Wade smiled while rubbing his back and pulling air through his teeth. Uncle Wade was right here with him in this world behind his eyelids, but he would have also told him to take inventory one more time.

Nick sat up and considered his stock again. Sawed off, box of shells. Two buck knives. Handgun, three clips for the handgun, army bag. Since his release money was tight. The pawn shop would take about every item he had of Uncle Wade's. That would get a place to rent. He'd been squatting in their old apartment, but the heat was too much, and it was about that time when the landlord paid a visit. He had given Blair his uncle's military patches. Sharpshooter, combat engineer, and a few others he wasn't sure about. She seemed to appreciate it, and he knew Uncle Wade had a thing for her, even though he had never said much.

Nick took one more look and then placed each item into the army bag, lay back one last time. He closed his eyes. *Rehab actually helped.* He took it as a way out of prison early, but it was nice being able to think clearly, even if some of that thinking gave him nightmares. To balance out the nightmares, he daydreamed. Behind closed eyes he could imagine what he needed into existence exactly as he wanted it.

He's on the school bus and Uncle Wade is standing outside the window. The bus hasn't pulled out yet and Uncle Wade is punching the air and ducking his head and giving him a thumbs up sign and then a big smile. The big smile says do not worry. It says you can do this. It says sometimes people say mean things like calling him Brown Bottle, and then sometimes people have to do mean things. His smile says a lot and so do his punching hands and his hooked thumbs, and before everything else it can possibly say, it says the thing Nick needs most. The big smile says I love you.

About the Author

Sheldon Lee Compton was born, raised, and continues to survive in Pike County, Kentucky, the commonwealth's easternmost tip. He lives there with his wife, Heather, and two children, Tyler Lee and Natalie Grace. He has worked as a coal miner, journalist, public relations specialist, short order cook, college professor, speech writer, and carpenter. His writing career started at the age of fourteen as an opinion columnist for the local newspaper.

A graduate of Spalding University's MFA program in Louisville, he is the author of the short story collections *The Same Terrible Storm* and *Where Alligators Sleep*. He has been nominated for the Chaffin Award for Excellence in Appalachian Writing and was a finalist for both the Gertrude Stein Fiction Award and the Still Fiction Award in 2012. His work was most recently included as a finalist in Queen's Ferry Press's anthology *The Best Small Fictions 2015*. In addition to his own work, he founded and edits the online journal *Revolution John* and is a former associate editor of the acclaimed literary journal *Night Train*.

Though a lifelong Kentuckian, he is an avid fan of the Atlanta Braves and considers baseball to be the purest sport yet imagined.

RECENT BOOKS BY BOTTOM DOG PRESS

HARMONY SERIES

Stolen Child: A Novel by Suzanne Kelly, 338 pgs. $18

The Canary : A Novel by Michael Loyd Gray, 196 pgs. $18

On the Flyleaf: Poems by Herbert Woodward Martin, 106 pgs. $16

The Harmonist at Nightfall: Poems of Indianab
by Shari Wagner, 114 pgs. $16

Painting Bridges: A Novel by Patricia Averbach, 234 pgs. $18

Ariadne & Other Poems by Ingrid Swanberg, 120 pgs. $16

The Search for the Reason Why: New and Selected Poems
by Tom Kryss, 192 pgs. $16

Kenneth Patchen: Rebel Poet in America
by Larry Smith, Revised 2nd Edition, 326 pgs. Cloth $28

Selected Correspondence of Kenneth Patchen,
Edited with introduction by Allen Frost, Paper $18/ Cloth $28

Awash with Roses: Collected Love Poems of Kenneth Patchen
Eds. Laura Smith and Larry Smith
With introduction by Larry Smith, 200 pgs. $16

HARMONY COLLECTIONS AND ANTHOLOGIES

d.a.levy and the mimeograph revolution
Eds. Ingrid Swanberg and Larry Smith, 276 pgs. $20

Come Together: Imagine Peace
Eds. Ann Smith, Larry Smith, Philip Metres, 204 pgs. $16

Evensong: Contemporary American Poets on Spirituality
Eds. Gerry LaFemina and Chad Prevost, 240 pgs. $16

America Zen: A Gathering of Poets
Eds. Ray McNiece and Larry Smith, 224 pgs. $16

Family Matters: Poems of Our Families
Eds. Ann Smith and Larry Smith, 232 pgs. $16

Breathing the West: Great Basin Poems
by Liane Ellison Norman, 80 pgs. $16

Maggot : A Novel by Robert Flanagan, 262 pgs. $18

American Poet: A Novel by Jeff Vande Zande, 200 pgs. $18

The Way-Back Room: Memoir of a Detroit Childhood
by Mary Minock, 216 pgs. $18

Strangers in America: A Novel by Erika Meyers, 140 pgs. $16

Riders on the Storm: A Novel by Susan Streeter Carpenter, 404 pgs. $18

Landscape with Fragmented Figures: A Novel
by Jeff Vande Zande, 232 pgs. $16

The Big Book of Daniel: Collected Poems
by Daniel Thompson, 340 pgs. Paper $18/ Cloth $22;

RECENT BOOKS BY BOTTOM DOG PRESS

APPALACHIAN WRITING SERIES

Brown Bottle: A Novel by Sheldon Lee Compton, 162 pgs. $18
A Small Room with Trouble on My Mind by Michael Henson, 164 pgs. $18
Drone String: Poems by Sherry Cook Stanforth, 92 pgs. $16
Voices from the Appalachian Coalfields by Mike Yarrow and Ruth Yarrow,
Photos by Douglas Yarrow, 152 pgs. $17
Wanted: Good Family by Joseph G. Anthony, 212 pgs. $18
Sky Under the Roof: Poems by Hilda Downer, 126 pgs. $16
Green-Silver and Silent: Poems by Marc Harshman, 90 pgs. $16
The Homegoing: A Novel by Michael Olin-Hitt,180 pgs. $18
*She Who Is Like a Mare: Poems of Mary Breckinridge and
the Frontier Nursing Service* by Karen Kotrba, 96 pgs. $16
Smoke: Poems by Jeanne Bryner, 96 pgs. $16
Broken Collar: A Novel by Ron Mitchell, 234 pgs. $18
The Pattern Maker's Daughter: Poems
by Sandee Gertz Umbach, 90 pages $16
The Free Farm: A Novel by Larry Smith, 306 pgs. $18
Sinners of Sanction County: Stories by Charles Dodd White, 160 pgs. $17
Learning How: Stories, Yarns & Tales by Richard Hague, 216 pgs. $18
The Long River Home: A Novel
by Larry Smith, 230 pgs. cloth $22; paper $16
Eclipse: Stories by Jeanne Bryner, 150 pgs. $16

APPALACHIAN ANTHOLOGIES

Appalachia Now: Short Stories of Contemporary Appalachia
Eds. Charles Dodd White and Larry Smith, 160 pgs. $18
Degrees of Elevation: Short Stories of Contemporary Appalachia
Eds. Charles Dodd White and Page Seay, 186 pgs. $18

Bottom Dog Press, Inc.
P.O. Box 425 /Huron, Ohio 44839
http://smithdocs.net